# The Connection

L.A. Lyons

CHARLES TOWNE PUBLISHING
CHARLESTON, SOUTH CAROLINA
2012

The sale of this book without its cover is unauthorized. If you purchased this book without a cover, you should be aware that it was reported to the publisher as "unsold and destroyed." Neither the author nor the publisher has received payment for the sale of this "stripped book."

Charles Towne Publishing
Charleston, South Carolina 29401
**www.charlestownepublish.com**

Copyright © 2012 by L.A. Lyons

This book is a work of fiction. Names, characters, places, and incidents are products of the author's imagination or are used fictitiously. Any resemblance to actual events or locales or persons, living or dead, is entirely coincidental.

ISBN-13: **978-0615606774**
ISBN-10: **0615606776**

First Charles Towne Publishing edition April 2012

Manufactured in the United States of America

For information regarding special discounts on bulk purchases, please contact Charles Towne Publishing at
**accounts@charlestownepublish.com**

"To my family who has always given me the opportunity to dream"

*"We are better than we think and not quite what we want to be"*

- Nikki Giovanni

# The Connection

*The little boy is wearing the same green t-shirt with the ninja turtles on it, like he is every time I see him sitting in that same old sandbox in the park. I squint against the raging sun to make out his face, but like always, I can never get a good look. There are a few other kids playing on the jungle gym and swing set, but he is always just playing by himself in the sandbox.*

*He looks happy enough, even though he's not playing with any friends or siblings. He seems content.*

*Suddenly, I find myself soaring high above a tree line. I look down and marvel at how green the trees are. The sun is bright and refreshing, but not overwhelming. I am weaving along the water line below. I'm not sure if it's a river or a lake, but it sure is beautiful. I can barely make out the ant-like people below, but I can hear the roar of boat engines. I hear their laughter. I breathe in the cold, mountain air, and I feel at home.*

## CHAPTER 1: SUBURBIA

I woke up from my usual dream. I used to get upset wondering who that little boy in the park was, but now I don't worry about it much. I've had the same dream for as long as I can remember, and I've grown accustomed to watching him play without ever really knowing anything about him.

I've just started having the last part of my dream in the past two months or so. I think it's because I'm planning on going to the University of Colorado at Boulder next year for college. Yup, I'm getting out of dreary old Pittsburgh finally!

A few months ago it was early April, and I still hadn't solidified which college I'd be attending next year. My final choices were the University of Colorado, my hometown University of Pittsburgh, and George Washington University, down in Washington, D.C.

I really did not want to go to Pitt. For the past four years in high school, all I've done is dream about getting out of Pittsburgh, although I'm not exactly sure why. I like my mom, but like all moms she can get on my last teenage nerve, and I have a good group of friends, but there's just something in me that wants to run away from here. Too many kids in my class were going to Pitt, and even though it is a great academic school, it wasn't right for me.

My dad made me apply to George Washington because he lives in D.C. now, and he thought it would be a good idea to go to school near him and his new family. I say his new family because, yes, I know, I'm his family, I'm his daughter, but after he and my mom got divorced when I was four, he moved to D.C., met a nice lady named Janet, married her, and inherited her two children. My stepsiblings, Josh and Kim, are nice enough, and we're pretty close in age. Actually, I really like them. I like Janet too, but I could never leave my mom here by herself while I go gallivanting with my dad's new family. I could never do that to her. So, George Washington was pretty much not an option.

Anyway, that's why I applied to the University of Colorado. It was so far away and that seemed super appealing. My dreams of this amazing wilderness seemed to lure me in. I looked up pictures of the university and they matched almost perfectly with the images from in dreams. I took that as a positive sign, sent in my housing deposit, and secured my spot in the University of Colorado at Boulder's class of 2015!

Yes, I was still leaving my mom, and she'd be here in Pittsburgh alone, but at least I wasn't joining up with a new family in D.C., and although she'd never say it, I know she was relieved I wasn't going to college near Dad.

So each night, when I have these dreams about the University of Colorado, I get more and more excited to get out there and start the next chapter of my life. You would think I'm a huge wilderness geek for choosing this school, and because of the dreams I've been having, but I'm not. I like the wilderness, and I'm a pretty adventurous person, but something about the scenery just draws me to it. Maybe I will become a big nature buff, who knows? All I know is that I'm ready to be out of this stepford, suburban Township.

I live in an upscale neighborhood, about twenty minutes south of Pittsburgh, where everyone knows everyone else's business. Moms don't have to work because their husbands make bank, so they get to spend their days playing tennis, shopping, and lunching at the country club. Every family looks like the perfect cookie cutter family from the outside, but most are reeling on the inside. They aren't happy at all. This has been my first real life lesson--- that everything is not what it seems.

My high school is ranked number one in the state for academics and athletics. Go Panthers! Not. I am not a sports fan at all. The most athletic thing I've done has been chasing a neighborhood dog after he escaped and went on a joy run last summer. I ran for a solid three minutes and almost died. That pretty much sums up my athletic prowess.

I do care about my education though, as much as an 18-year-old can, I guess. I get straight A's---strike that, I can't lie---I've had one single, solitary B in my high school career. I will never forgive Ms. Betris, my tenth grade English teacher, for that one. I actually like learning. My favorite subject is English, which is ironic since that's the only subject I received a B in, but nonetheless, I still tout it as my favorite. It's probably because I absolutely love to read. I love reading adventures and mystery novels the most. I think because I've lived in Pittsburgh my entire life, and have barely traveled, adventure novels really speak to me. I'm jealous of those stories. Someday I will have stories of my own. They will start next year in Colorado.

This place isn't all bad though. I make it out to be worse than it really is. I do have some good friends, namely my best friend, Natalie. We've been best friends since middle school. Natalie is the most popular girl in our grade; she's the captain of varsity cheerleading and dates the captain of the varsity lacrosse team, Kyle. I'm not a big Kyle fan, but I love Natalie like the sibling I never had, and I put up with Kyle because I love Natalie. To complete our Lizzie McGuire best friend club, we have Nate. Nate's been our third wheel since freshman year. Nate is more like me than Natalie. He's not really into sports, and is kind of nerdy, but he is a really hilarious guy. He thinks he is going to be some kind of forensic scientist when he grows up, but I know whatever he does he will somehow make an impact on this big world. His mom isn't really thrilled with any of his current career paths because she is worried more about his economic future than anything else. Luckily Nate didn't inherit his parents' pompousness, and he balances out both Natalie and me.

That's why Nate seemed like the perfect choice for a prom date. Even though we didn't have an affinity for the in-crowd at school, and we were both kind of book nerds, we were still social. Prom would be the last hoorah with these shallow people that I hoped I'd never see again. At least until our coveted 10-year reunion, where I would show up in a limo with Nate and Natalie--- all three of us being uber successful--- and the rest of our classmates would be drooling all over themselves with jealousy. It will be perfect. But for now, we would have to settle for having a great prom night.

Natalie has been saying, "It's going to be epic, Kennedy, trust me," for what seems like all year now. Of course, Natalie is going with Kyle. Big whoop. At least I only had to stomach him for a few more months because I'm sure they will break up once they get to college. That sounds mean, but it will be better for her in the long run. They are both going to Penn State---

another big shocker--- because something like a quarter of our graduating class is going there. I still think Natalie will meet some other, more interesting, college guy, and will finally have the guts to cut Kyle loose once and for all, at least that's what I hope.

Today was finally the day, and after my two usual dreams, I feel like I'm right on track for a great prom day/night.

*♪ ♪ I gotta feeling that tonight's gonna be a good night*
*That tonight's gonna be a good night*

*That tonight's gonna be a good good night ♪ ♪*

I snatched up my cell phone that was playing what had to be the most annoying song of the past decade, Black Eyed Peas, "Tonight is Gonna Be a Good Night." It could only be Natalie who had programmed this ring tone on my phone for this specific day. I wanted to punch her, but I couldn't help but smile as I saw her picture on my screen as I answered her call.

# CHAPTER 2: PROM PREP

"I cannot believe it's finally prom night!" Natalie screeched, as the lady at the nail salon shuffled us back to our pedicure stations. Natalie's mom had arranged a spa day for us months ago. I think Natalie's mom still dreams about her prom night. She always told us that she was a late bloomer in high school, which translates into that she was not very pretty, or popular, and didn't get asked to the prom.

She was always a girly girl and grew up dreaming about prom, so the fact that she never got to go practically destroyed her. But Natalie's mom really is a good person, and if you believe in karma, which I do, she got some pretty good stuff later in life. She must have come into her own in college at Penn State, because that's where she met Natalie's dad. He was the starting linebacker at Penn State. They fell in love, got married, and he was drafted to the NFL. Sounds like a dream, right?

Natalie's life is kind of like a dream in that way. Her parents are both very good looking, her dad is a retired NFL player, they have loads of money, and both love their daughter very much. They couldn't be happier with her choice of college, their alma mater, but they could do without her choice of boyfriends. Her mother doesn't really approve, but her father tries to give Kyle the benefit of the doubt because he says he sees part of himself in Kyle, and he thinks Kyle will grow out of it like he did. I doubt it, but again, not my choice.

We assumed our positions atop our pedicure chairs, with our feet nicely set into the soothing hot water, armed with piles of US Weekly, Cosmo, and Entertainment Weekly. Natalie frequented this establishment much more than I did, but I'm not going to lie and say I didn't enjoy a bi-monthly pedicure here and there.

"Kennedy, are you so siked for tonight? It's going to be amazing. It's going to be a good, good night!"

"I have been meaning to talk to you about that. Nat, when did you change my ring tone to that terrible Black Eyed Peas song? You know I hate it!" I responded.

"Ha ha, you love it! I did it at lunch yesterday when you were getting your soda. I knew it would be perfect for today."

"Right. I took it off already, just so you know. But yes, I am excited for tonight; it's going to be fun. And the dinner is going to be amazing, and then afterwards we can all come back to my house for all night movies. We can go rent them after we leave here," I said.

"Oh," Natalie quickly interjected, "I forgot to tell you. Kyle's buddy, Dax, from the lacrosse team, is having a big after party at his family's cabin in Deep Creek, Maryland. We can all spend the night, it'll be so fun!"

"Since when?" I asked, defensively. I was really looking forward to movie night with my best friends.

"I don't know. Kyle actually just mentioned it to me this morning before I picked you up."

"Who all is going? You know I don't like Kyle's friends on the lacrosse team. They're all so," I stalled, not wanting to hurt Natalie's feelings.

"They're all so what?" she questioned.

"They're all jerks. You know it, Natalie. Kyle's not even that nice, but I accept him, I don't want to get into it. But his friends, they're not very nice. They drink too much. They grope girls. They say derogatory things. Not exactly my version of a fun after prom party."

"Oh." Natalie sounded a little hurt and dejected by my statement.

Now I felt bad. Natalie knows how I feel about Kyle, and deep down, I think she knows she deserves much better. And we've talked a lot about how she doesn't really like his friends either, but she puts up with them because of Kyle. I never thought she'd want to go to this type of party. Even though Natalie was gorgeous and smart, and the most popular girl in our grade, she still had the usual teenage girl confidence issues.

"Nat, I didn't mean it like that. I'm sorry, I'll ask Nate and see if he wants to go," I said to her before she got any more upset. After all, it was our one and only prom night.

"You will?" Natalie's face instantly brightened up, and she resumed skimming through her copy of *US Weekly*.

"Yeah, I'll text him now. Do we have to stay overnight though?" I asked.

"Um, I think you will want to. It's like two hours away, I think."

I forgot how far away Deep Creek Lake was from here. Natalie was right, it was a little under two hours away. I haven't been there since middle school when our friend Daisy had her 12th birthday party at her family's cabin. We call them cabins because it sounds charming, but these houses are far from the typical rustic cabin. These are multi-million dollar, luxurious, highly coveted, lake houses.

"Oh, I forgot. You're right. That's a pretty long drive for one night, don't ya think?" I asked, hoping she'd agree and we could get to have our movie marathon tonight after all.

"I mean, I guess, but it'll be so much fun. This is our only prom, and our only after-prom party. Come on, Kennedy, pleeeeeease."

I hate it when she whines. I shrugged, smiled, and picked up my phone and texted Nate.

"OK, I texted Nate. If he says he'll go, then I will too. I'm definitely not going alone only to be ditched by you and Kyle, deal?" I asked, hoping some other barrier would prevent me from actually going.

"Deal," Natalie agreed.

The rest of the mani-pedi combo seemed to fly by. I read some articles on my favorite celebrities, and thoroughly enjoyed myself. Even though I am a self-labeled geek, I still love celebrity gossip and news. I read about Kim Kardashian's engagement twice. Her engagement ring was flawless, and the size of a boulder. Natalie is the type of girl that will get a ring like that, not me. I'm not even sure I'd want something that big and gaudy, but it sure is beautiful.

I also caught up on my prom fashions. After looking at the ideal dress for each body type, I wasn't sure that my very plain, black halter-top dress was going to turn any heads, but I'm okay with that.

I've become used to being the sidekick. Natalie never treats me that way, but she is always the center of attention when we're at school or at social events. It's not her fault; she really is beautiful and very charismatic. That's probably part of the reason I like her so much. I'm sure she doesn't love the fact that I'm such a nerd, but she always makes me feel good about myself. She supports me, and sticks up for me, and is an overall good, genuine person. I'm sure her tangerine, strapless dress is going to drop jaws. I don't doubt it for a second. Her blonde hair seems even brighter against her end of spring tan she has going on, courtesy of a spring break trip to Panama City, and a package at the local tanning salon. Plus she's always sporting a genuine smile that draws people to her. Part of the reason I picked a black dress, besides the fact that I think it is timeless, is because I abhor tanning salons, and have the typical Pittsburgh pale, white skin. I have it a little better than most though because at least my skin has an olive tint year round, saving me from completely looking like Casper. My dark brown hair does nothing to jazz up my appearance either, but that's the hand I've been dealt.

"Kennedy, your nails look so nice!" Natalie beamed.

"You think? They're pretty plain," I shrugged.

"No way, I really like that silver color, it'll go really great with your dress and shoes, you'll see!" This is exactly the type of compliment I was talking about. Natalie is unfailingly kind.

"Yours look good too, Nat."

"Thanks, but I know you hate the French pedicure."

She couldn't have been more right. I have this weird pet peeve that toes should definitely not look like fingers. Some people have abnormally long, skinny toes that, unfortunately, make them look like wanna-be fingers, but when people go that extra step and get a French pedicure on their toes, I freak out. Natalie did just this.

"Ha, I wasn't going to say anything, but now that you mention it…"

"You're so weird, Kennedy, but that's why I love you."

We walked out to Natalie's car, a 2012 Audi A4, an early graduation gift. Her parents upgraded her from her raggedy, old 2009 Volkswagen Jetta. What an eyesore that thing was. I, however, drive around in a modest 2005 Honda Civic. I'm not complaining--- I'm fortunate too, I'm not denying that--- but some people, like Natalie, live a charmed life. And a lot of those people happen to live in our township.

"Where to now?" I asked, honestly not knowing what the plan was for the rest of the day.

"My mom got us massages at the country club, after lunch," Natalie informed me.

"That's really nice of her. Where are we getting lunch?" I asked.

"At the club with my mom. She's already there waiting for us."

These were times I wished that Natalie's mom and my mom were closer. They got along fine, I mean they have been dealing with each other for years because we were best friends, but they by no means were best friends. I let my mind drift to how nice it would be to have my mom with us today. I thought about asking Natalie if I could ask my mom to join us, but got distracted by my phone vibrating.

"Who is it?" Natalie asked as she saw me glance down at my phone.

"It's Nate."

"Did he respond about Deep Creek? What did he say? Tell!" Natalie squeaked again, as she does often when she gets excited.

*Nate: I guess that's ok. I'd rather just watch movies like we said we were going to do.*

I couldn't tell Natalie this, so I stalled while I wrote back to him.

*Me: Ya, I know. Me too. I tried to tell Nat, but she really wants to go. I feel bad. Just go, and we'll do movie night another night, k?*

I couldn't believe I was actually attempting to persuade Nate into going when I didn't even want to go. But Natalie seemed really excited, and she has spent enough time with Nate and I, being quote unquote losers, on Friday nights watching old movies. Sometimes I felt like we were keeping her from the life she was supposed to live--- you know the duties of being the most popular girl in school. She didn't seem to mind all that much, but at times like tonight, you could tell she really craved the party scene, and I figured we *do* only have one prom night, what the hell?

"Seriously, what's up? What did Nate say?" She asked again.

"I think he is OK with it," was all I could come up with right now.

"You think? What did he say?"

*Nate: Ya, ok, you're right. We'll make the best of it. Should I bring my portable DVD player, just in case?* ☺

I loved Nate for saying things just like that. Not *love* love like that, just love like my best guy friend. That actually was a smart idea too because neither of us are big drinkers, and since we can't stand anybody that's going to be there besides Natalie, we probably will want to sneak off and watch a movie.

*Me: BRING IT! See you soon!*

"He's coming. I'm coming. We're all going," I told Natalie.

To this, she gave out the loudest yelp in history, seriously. She almost ran a red light, and then slammed on the brakes. Her mood instantly flung into a whole other zone. She turned up the radio and as luck would have it, and much to my dismay, her theme song for the day was now blaring through her Bose speakers.

"Tonight's gonna be a good, good niiiiiiight woooooohoooo," Natalie sang.

"Shoot me now," I replied back.

Natalie just turned up the radio and drove on to the country club.

## CHAPTER 3: PROM

"Kennedy! Where are you? Are you almost ready?" My mom's voice echoed up our foyer staircase and into my room. I thought I had shut my door, but I must have left it open before I lay down for my pre-prom nap. All that pampering and country clubbing wiped me out. The life of a privileged young member of society is rough, let me tell you. Then add in my mom's third degree questioning about my manicure, pedicure, and lunch with Natalie and her mother and it all had left me even more exhausted. I was never going to make it through tonight without a little power nap.

"Kennedy! Nate will be here in five minutes, I'm coming up." I could hear my mother's footsteps up the hardwood stairs, and I jumped out of bed. Five minutes? How long had I slept for? I had set my alarm for 3:30p.m., which would have given me ample time to attempt to style my hair, do my makeup, and slide on my drab dress.

I looked at my cell: 5:15 p.m.! What? I was screwed. My phone alarm must have messed up. Looks like tonight is not going to be such a good night after all, Fergie.

"Kennedy, what on earth?" my mother exclaimed.

She loved saying cliché mom things like "what on earth."

"It's OK, I've got this under control," I tried to fake it.

"No, you certainly do not. Look at you, you're a mess!"

"Oh thanks, Mom. You're such a confidence booster," I whined back.

"Well, what do you expect? Nate is probably on his way by now and you've just woken up. I don't even know where to start?"

"I do. Just go downstairs, and I'll be done in fifteen minutes. Nate and I will just be a few minutes late to pictures at Natalie's, no big deal," I said, although I knew it would be a monumental deal to Natalie. She had this night planned down to the second, and my being fifteen minutes late would not benefit anyone.

"Here, just let me help you," she said as she grabbed my hairbrush and searched through my sorry excuse for a makeup drawer in my bathroom.

"No, Mom, really, it'll go faster if you just let me do this myself," I said.

"Why do you do that? You always push me away. Let me help you for God's sake."

With this, I knew I had hurt my mom's feelings. I was her only daughter, her only child at all, and I wasn't letting her in on any part of this special coming of age ritual that we fondly call prom. She hadn't gone to get her nails done with us, and she didn't even get lunch like Natalie's mother did.

I caved. "Alright, can you please get my bobby pins from that drawer there, some bronzer, eyeliner, and mascara, and I'll go wash my face really fast, and we'll go from there."

"Got it," she replied with a smile that spread across her whole face.

A few seconds later, my mom had gathered all the necessary tools and sat on my bed waiting. I quickly washed my face, grabbed my dress from hanging on the shower rod, and went back into my room.

I started to slip off my sweats when my mom stopped me.

"You don't put on your dress first; you don't want to get any makeup on it. That goes last. Come here, sit."

"Mom, you're not doing my hair, that's where I draw the line," I strongly said.

"But…"

I interrupted her, "No buts, Mom. You can help touch it up with the bobby pins, that's it."

I gave my hair a quick brush through, shook my head out a bit, and bent at the waist, letting my long, brown hair dangle in front of my face. I had absolutely no idea what I was going to do. The one thing I did have going for me was that my hair was long and thick. It always somehow looked pretty nice in a ponytail, even if it was just for lounging around the house. My ponytails were top of the line.

I remembered seeing a hairstyle in the magazine this morning with a little poof at the front. Jersey Shore style, I think, but not as crazy and attention seeking. That would be easy.

The poof turned out pretty good, surprisingly, then I quickly brushed the rest back into a pony, and asked my mom to turn on the straightener to give my ponytail a once over. She seemed happy enough with the task, she just likes to help, and I realize this. I put it in my memory bank to cut her a little more slack, especially this summer before I abandon her for Colorado.

I do feel bad about it, still.

Once the hair was situated, I moved to the make-up, which was really not my scene. I quickly brushed on the bronzer, since my pale skin was doing me no favors. At least my freckles hid just how white my skin really was right now. Then came the eyeliner and mascara. I let Nadene help with mascara. I call her by her first name sometimes because she always used to joke with my friends that they should call her Nadene instead of Mrs. Clark. So I just started calling her that. Some parents look at me with disgust when I say it, they must think I'm being rude, or a smart ass, but I'm not, not really. My mom doesn't mind so what do they care?

My face didn't look half bad for just waking up, and I walked over to grab the dress. Just then, we heard the doorbell.

"That must be Nate. Can you go let him in, Mom? I'm nearly done here anyhow. I'll be down in two minutes, I promise."

"Sure, honey," she said, just before she paused in the frame of my doorway out of my room.

"What?" I asked, staring back at her.

"You are so grown up. You look beautiful. I love you."

My mom had no problem being so honest and lovey-dovey. I definitely didn't inherit that gene from her. I guess I'm more like my dad in that way. He isn't one to really let his feelings flow, but I'm okay with that. I know my parents love me, especially my mom, and I think--- I hope--- she knows how much I love her too, even though I don't verbalize it as much as she does, or as much as I should.

"Thanks, Mom. Love you too," I said back, really meaning it. It was going to be harder to leave this lady than I had thought. It's for the best, though.

With that, she turned and Nate rang the doorbell again

as I heard her go down the stairs.

    I shut my door and slipped on my dress. At first I thought that I had somehow grabbed the wrong dress. It was the same black as I remember buying from Macy's a month earlier, but this one had silver sparkles around the neckline. Those weren't there before. They were nice though. They really accentuated it nicely. Accentuated? Eww, who am I? I've read too many *Cosmo* magazines today. It did look nice, though. My mom must have done this without me knowing. This was a huge risk for her, she knows how picky I am with everything, that's why I pick such simple things like this plain, black dress. This was just another thoughtful thing my mom has done for me, and finally, this time, I appreciated it.

    I grabbed my shoes and ran downstairs to find Nate and his mom sitting on the couches in our living room.

    "Wow, you look really nice, Kennedy," Nate blurted out.

    "Thanks, Nate," I replied.

    "You really do, honey. Do you like the alterations to the dress?" My mom asked.

    "Mom, I really, really do. Thank you. They look great. Thanks."

    "Kennedy, darling, you look fantastic. You and Nathan will be such a dashing couple tonight," Nate's mom chimed in.

    "Thank you." I said, then held my tongue, Nate's mom wasn't my favorite person. Her backhanded compliment of "tonight" was her way of showing her displeasure at us even being considered a couple for the night, and that we certainly would not be a couple after our brief outing at prom. Not that Nate and I would ever even want to be considered a couple, but the fact that his mom thought that I wasn't good enough for him always made me mad. Not that Nate isn't a good catch; it's just that she only thinks in terms of money. Nate's father is a chemist who works at Bayer and makes a ton of money. My family is well off, but we're not in the same league with Natalie or Nate's family, and pairing someone like me with Nate was not desirable to his mother. Forget that I have a 3.95 GPA, am going to a great school, and am a genuinely good person. That doesn't matter. So I stick to "Thank you," and move on.

A few pictures were taken. A few tears were cried by my mother. Then Nate and I were on our way to Natalie's to take a few pictures with her and Kyle.

Nate really did look great tonight. His usual casual jeans and drab polo shirt were replaced by a sharp, grey, three-piece suit. It seemed like Nate was filling out his suit nicely. He somehow transitioned from awkward and lanky geek to a suave young man. I never realized how much I liked guys in vests until right then. Nate slipped off his jacket as we got into his car to drive over to Natalie's. His grey suit was complimented by a light blue shirt that really made him look handsome. He's my best friend so I can call him handsome. He did look good though, and for the first time, I was a bit jealous of the college girl who would really get to know Nate, and get to call him her own. I just hope I liked her.

"You really do look good, Nate," I said to him.

"Thanks. My mom made me try on a bazillion suits and shirts and ties, and we finally decided on this. I think it's a cool combo," he said back casually.

"I totally agree. I like the grey! You got a haircut, too!" Nate's usual overgrown, curly mop of hair had been weed-whacked down to an acceptable length where it was longer than most, but it curled at the edges so you could properly see his face. His blue shirt matched his cool baby blues perfectly. He really did look good tonight. Maybe tonight wouldn't be as bad as I thought, waking up embarrassingly late from my nap.

I told Nate how my alarm had failed to go off and how I had ten minutes to get ready. He is always impressed with how much I get done in short periods of time.

When we pulled up to Natalie's, everyone was already outside on the front lawn. We were only a few minutes late. I hoped she didn't freak out.

"Hi Natalie, I'm sorry, I was late picking Kennedy up," Nate offered up an excuse, being so gentleman-like and taking the blame when it was actually my fault.

Natalie waved eagerly for us to come over by her and Kyle, shouting, "It's ok, perfect timing, Kyle just got here too." Saved by the Kyle.

Natalie's parents were both outside, chatting it up with Kyle's parents. Kyle had wandered away from Natalie and was throwing a nerf football to Natalie's little brother. Kyle motioned like he was going over to tackle Natalie's little brother, and Natalie screamed and shuffled over to him as best she could in her mermaid tight, tangerine dress, and grabbed him by the ear and reigned him back in. Typical Kyle, he's literally an 8-year-old inside an 18-year-old's body.

"Mom, Dad, get the cameras, let's get some pictures," Natalie instructed her parents.

I tried to block out the next few minutes to avoid the uncomfortable act of prom picture taking. I had been through the drill a few times with Natalie at other school dances, mostly during freshman year, because after that, I had boycotted going to any others. You waste so much money on a new dress, because no one in this community can borrow each other's dress--- that's completely out of the question--- then you drop a good chunk on pampering for the day, hair, makeup, etc. Add in the ridiculously expensive dinner, where teenagers imitate their parents, going to the most expensive, snotty restaurants that overcharge you for a small plate of food that still leaves you hungry, forcing you to go through the Sonic drive thru before you even get to the dance. And, I almost forgot, the limo. You can't go in your car or your parents' car--- even if it is an Audi, Mercedes, or BMW. No way, José. By the time you add up all this money, you have spent a small fortune on a two hour dance with somebody you probably don't even like. No thanks.

Finally, the pictures were done, and the stretch H2 Hummer Limo pulled up in front of Natalie's house. A bit extravagant for four people, but that's how we roll here. Kyle's parents paid for the limo. We were all going to pitch in, but I threw a fit. No way was I going to ask my mom to pay toward a limo for four people! It must have gotten back to Kyle's parents, and they just said they would pay for it all, no problem. The truth was, it was no problem for them, so I didn't feel bad for them footing the bill. I could have walked to dinner, I wouldn't care.

The limo ride to the ridiculously expensive and uppity restaurant was a bit awkward, like it always is when it's us three Kyle. I have to give it to Kyle, it can't be easy dating a girl like Natalie in the first place, because she is high maintenance and tons of other guys are always after her, but also because he always has to put up with Nate and me. We give him a hard time, yank his chain, and talk about things he couldn't be less interested in, but at least he tries to be polite and get along with us most of the time, and I guess that's all we really can ask for.

As predicted, dinner was expensive and small, so we stopped by the Sonic drive-thru on the way, and finally felt nourished. Typical. The actual prom was pretty nice, and once we made our way into the banquet room of the posh hotel, it wasn't half bad. The worst part was getting out of the limo and onto the red carpet. We're not famous, but most of my classmates tend to think they are that important. It's a tradition here at my school. Every prom has a red carpet that everyone walks down to get into the hotel. The carpet is complete with side rails that parents stand behind, eagerly awaiting a chance to catch a glimpse of their son or daughter approaching. You hear, "Look here, smile, great," about a million times. I told Nadene not to come, but I wasn't surprised to see her there, next to Natalie's mother, camera in hand. For a second, you actually forget you are an 18-year-old high school student, and not Kim Kardashian. Good thing it only took 30 seconds to walk that damn carpet.

The hotel was all ours for the night, everything except the rooms. Kids were forbidden from renting rooms, and the parents were not allowed to rent them for their children either. But the rest of the hotel, lobby, banquet rooms, everything was ours. It was decorated nice, and I don't really care about that kind of stuff, but it looked nice.

Everything went pretty well. We danced a little, drank some punch that may or may not have been spiked, talked at the table, made fun of people dancing, and had a good time for the three hours we were there.

Natalie and Kyle only fought once, that I saw at least, which was less than I would have figured for them. Nate and I were dancing to a song by local rap artist, Wiz Khalifa, who my school must have paid a hefty price to get him to come perform at our prom, when I saw Kyle get pushed back by another guy from our school.

Natalie and Kyle had been dancing, and Kyle's buddy Dax, whose cabin we are going to tonight, looked at Natalie funny, Kyle said. Kyle pushed Dax, and then other guys responded. Everything settled down, and I saw Natalie and Kyle kissing seconds later. Not shocking at all.

Time seemed to go by pretty fast, and before I knew it, they were announcing that prom was ending in a few minutes. We hadn't exactly planned out the day very well, because the limo was waiting take us back to Natalie's house, but now we were going to Dax's cabin in Deep Creek. Kyle unrealistically asked if the limo could drive a bunch of us to Deep Creek, but his dad immediately nixed the idea. The limo took us back to Natalie's as planned, and Nate volunteered to drive us to Dax's cabin in Deep Creek. Really, Kyle should have drove, but he had snuck in a couple airplane bottles of tequila to the dance, and had a few cups of the spiked punch. In any case, he could not drive, so Nate, always the gentleman, volunteered.

The four of us, along with a small duffle Natalie had packed earlier, piled into the Audi and set the GPS to the cabin's address.

# CHAPTER 4: AFTER PARTY

    The drive went by pretty fast, thanks to Natalie's post-prom CD mix that she made earlier. That girl seriously thinks of everything, and I was thankful not to have to hear that damn Black Eyed Peas song one more time, and Natalie knew not to press my buttons by putting it on the CD. We all jammed out to Beyonce, Justin Timberlake, Kanye, Pink, and of course, our hometown boy and prom performer, Wiz Khalifa. The two hours flew by, and before we knew it we were pulling up to Dax's family cabin.

    It was gorgeous. Seriously, it was like something out of a magazine that you only dream of being able to actually see, let alone stay in. Sadly, as all the kids unloaded their cars, I could hear some kids bitching that the cabin wasn't right on the water, so ungrateful and bratty. Dax's family cabin was across the street from the lake, so you either had to drive, or walk the half-mile or so to get there. Although not lakefront, the cabin was tucked nicely into the side of an enormous mountain. The backside of the cabin was only feet away from the side of the mountain that sharply angled upward, leaving just enough room for the width of a car to park there, alongside the vast woods behind the house. It was beautiful, and reminded me a lot of my dreams I had been having of the Colorado landscape. I smiled and walked into the cabin with Natalie.

Natalie found Dax among the twenty or so other kids already there, and she asked him if we could pick out our rooms now. Dax could care less about room situations and just shrugged. He was more concerned with the placement of the three kegs being wheeled in.

Natalie took this as her cue to explore, and Nate and I followed. Who knew where Kyle was? Not us. We walked up the stairs to find four bedrooms, two on each side of the hallway. We quickly checked them out and picked the one with bunk beds, a single bed, and a couch. We figured this gave us the most room, so we plopped down our little duffle, and Nate safely hid his portable DVD player for later use.

I had stalled long enough and could hear all the commotion going on downstairs, so we decided to join the party. Natalie was a little more enthusiastic about it than Nate and I, but we put on our brave faces.

"Do you guys want a drink?" Natalie asked Nate and I.

I looked sideways at Nate and responded, "Um, no thanks, Natalie. Not for me. Nate?"

"Nah, not right now, maybe later," Nate said.

I knew Nate was just being nice; he didn't plan on having a drink later, but didn't want to ruin Natalie's party.

"Oh, you two are no fun at all. Come on, just something fun, or fruity, you pick," she persisted.

I thought quickly, and decided that I could at least take a drink and hold it in my hand, she would never know, and maybe she would stop bugging me. "Alright, fine. I'll have whatever you're going to make for yourself."

"Yay! I'll go fix something and find you guys. You sure you don't want a beer, Nate?" she asked once more.

I looked at Nate, hoping he would take my cue, but he didn't, "Nope."

"OK, fine, party pooper. Kennedy, I'll be right back with our drinks," she continued down the stairs to the kitchen where the line of bottles was quickly accumulating on the bar counter.

I told Nate, "You should have just said you'd take a beer and just hold it, to get her off your back for a second. I thought you were smart or something, come on."

"Yeah, you're right. I just don't understand why she has to push the drink on me so much. Who cares if we don't want to drink?" he asked.

"I don't think she cares that much," I said, "she just wants us to have fun, and she sees all these people drinking and thinks that's fun, but it's not."

We kept walking and Natalie found her way back to us. The living room was starting to fill up. The three kegs were placed strategically throughout the house. I saw one in the kitchen by the refrigerator, and one outside on the deck when I spun around. The third one's location was a mystery to me, and I could have cared less.

Natalie handed me a red solo cup filled with something that was a resemblance of a pink color.

"Cheers!" Natalie chirped as she clunked our cups together.

"Thanks," I replied.

Natalie took a big sip, made a sour face and shook her head from side to side, then realizing she made the "this drink is not very good" face, she smiled and watched me until I tried the drink.

I imagine I made a similar face when I took my first sip. It wasn't terrible, just way too sour to ever enjoy. I was just about to take another sip when Kyle came walking over and put his arm around Natalie. His timing was impeccable, for once.

"You guys are welcome," he said with all the cockiness he could muster.

"For what?" I protested.

"For letting your lame asses come to the popular kids party, that's why," he said.

"Oh, get over yourself, Kyle," I said, and started to continue to say we didn't even want to come, but I stopped myself because I didn't want to hurt Natalie's feelings, and that's where this conversation was going.

I spun away from Kyle and grabbed Nate's arm. We walked out to the deck to get some fresh air, but it was crowded with a bunch of kids struggling to get to the front of the keg line. I looked at my cell for the first time since we arrived at Deep Creek and went to text my mom. She had asked me to call or text her to let her know we were there and safe. I tried to call her, but the service apparently wasn't that great there. I tried for a few minutes to send a text, and finally it went through. At least she knew we were OK, because I'm sure she was at home, in her robe in the living room, sitting in her trusty, ratty, old recliner, reading one of her smutty novels, just waiting to hear that I arrived safely.

I started to feel bodies bump into mine at a more rapid rate, and decided it was time for us to venture back inside. Some lacrosse players, led by the host, Dax, had started up a beer pong game at the long picnic-like table in the middle of the living room. We stayed on the outside of the perimeter and watched for a few minutes before we became bored.

"Hey, let's try to find some music," I suggested to Nate.

"Yeah, I'll go back to the car and grab some CD's, you try to find a player," he replied.

I set off to look around the main living room floor, passed the beer pong game again, and then saw Kyle and Natalie in a side room, in what I guess you could call a study. I stopped for a second and was going to ask Kyle if he knew where a CD player was, but then thought better of it. But, just as I lingered for a second, I saw him raise his finger in front of Natalie's face, almost threateningly, and I took a step closer. Natalie must have heard and she turned to look at me.

"What the hell is going on, get away from her!" I said, my voice escalating.

"Mind your own damn business, Kennedy," Kyle yelled back.

"Who the hell do you think you are? You are nothing, Kyle, nothing. You don't treat people like this. Natalie, let's go." I'd had enough.

"No, Kennedy, it's OK, he was just upset, he wasn't doing anything to me, I promise," she said.

"Really? Because it looked like he was about to either spit in your face or hit you. Either way, it was nothing good. Let's go," I said once again.

"Get out of here, nobody wants you guys here, just leave already, dork," was Kyle's retort.

"Kyle, stop. Kennedy, honestly, it's fine," Natalie pleaded with me.

I walked over to her, grabbed her gently by her elbow and ushered her to the side. Just as we separated from Kyle, he stormed past us, pouting, and said, "Whatever." He's so mature.

I finally got out of Natalie what had really happened. The boys we saw in the living room must have just started up their game, and one of them misogynistically suggested that each team needed some hot cheerleaders to root for them. Since Kyle wasn't on either team yet, Natalie volunteered to cheer on Dax and his teammate. Natalie was just doing our school cheers, she says, and Dax asked her for a quick shoulder rub to loosen up his pong arm. She obliged, and Kyle must have seen from across the room. Nevermind that Kyle was downright flirting with another girl across the room. He stormed across the room, and I guess the innocent shoulder rub, plus the unscrupulous staring at Natalie at the dance, pushed Kyle over the edge. He went right up to Dax and chest bumped him, and when he made his point, he went after Natalie. He shuffled her into the study where I found them.

Natalie still insisted it was no big deal, and I went over, for the millionth time, that boys shouldn't treat girls the way Kyle treats her. It was like talking to a brick wall, but this time he came awfully close to becoming physical with her, and that's where I drew the line.

She assured me that he definitely would never touch her like that, and everything was fine.

"I still think we should leave. This is not a good scene. All those guys are drunk, beating up on each other, and those girls are oblivious. Nate will take us now, come on," I suggested, hoping that she would come with us.

"Nooooo. Kennedy, this is our one prom night, we drove all this way, give it a chance, please," she pleaded.

"OK, but listen, if I see him do that again, I'm going to deck him myself, and we are most definitely leaving, and you are never talking to him again, I promise you that."

"OK, Momma Kennedy. Let's go back out there. How's that drink I made you?" she switched subjects quickly.

We weren't back out with the group more than five minutes, and Nate and I lost Natalie. We found her a few minutes later, curled up on the corner of the couch with Kyle, snuggling. They looked like the happiest teenage couple in the world. I hoped to God that this would last, at least for the rest of the night. I was sick of patrolling the party, and was just about ready for portable movie night with Nate.

I took one more sip of my pink concoction for good measure, grabbed a bottle of water from the refrigerator, and retreated up to the room with Nate. As we walked up the stairs, I heard Natalie do a catcall, "Ow owww." Of course, everyone's attention turned to Nate and me in what looked like our effort to go to a room alone on prom night, which was not the case, but everyone there thought it was. Natalie always thought Nate and I would get together. We were perfect for each other, she always said. She really couldn't comprehend how a guy and a girl could be such platonic friends. "Not possible," she always protested, and after a while, I stopped trying to convince her. You win some and you lose some, and sometimes with Natalie, it was easier just to be silent and shake your head, and move on to the next topic.

"What movies did you bring?" I asked. I hoped he brought my favorite movie of all time to unwind to, *A League of Their Own*.

"I brought a couple of choices, you can pick. We've got *Old School* if you want something funny, *S.W.A.T.* if you want action, or *Friday the 13th* if you want scary," Nate said.

He certainly had a sense of humor.
"Are you kidding me right now? I didn't want to torture myself by watching a scary movie while we're in almost the exact

same type of setting where the killings took place, oh yeah, sure. Perfect Nate," I exclaimed, as I started to reach for *Old School*.

"Oh yeah, and I brought *A League of Their Own*, thought you might want that, too," he said with a smile.

Nate knew me so well. I snatched up my favorite movie, and popped it into the portable DVD player. I hopped into the bottom bunk, and Nate made a makeshift bed on the floor next to me so he could see the screen better.

I must have been more tired than I thought, or else Natalie's pink drink knocked me out, because all I saw from that movie was Kit Keller striking out, and then calling her wonderful sister Dottie a nag, and boom, I was out. I was oblivious to all of the noise downstairs.

*The little boy was standing in the sandbox this time, still with his trusty ninja turtles t-shirt on. He seemed to be looking around for someone. It was like I was him, and saw through his eyes now. We looked at the jungle gym, then over to the park benches nearby, back to the swing set, then over to where the parked cars were. I felt sad, overwhelmingly sad, and felt soft tears trickle down and rest on my cheeks. I sniffed my nose and threw down the plastic shovel in my right hand. I took a step forward, then another, then tripped on the outer wood of the sandbox and fell hard on my face into the soft, green grass. Seconds later, I was lifted high into the air, and then pressed hard into the chest of someone. This person was patting my head, my back, rubbing my arms and hands telling me I was OK. Next thing I knew, I was back on my own two feet and tearing off toward the seesaw.*

*Just as quick, I was soaring high above the tree line in Colorado. My flight was short lived, because after only a few seconds I was dropping from the sky fast. My breath was sucked back into my lungs, and I clenched every muscle in my body, bracing for impact. I dropped through the clouds, through the trees, amazingly not touching a single one, and gently parachuted down into the middle of a dense forest. I was just thankful that I hadn't plunged to an untimely death, and wasn't scared of where I was. It was dark outside, but it seemed like there was a light coming from somewhere far away, but it was bright enough to shed a little light so I could see. I was completely surrounded by incredibly tall trees, large stones, and rough terrain. It almost seemed like the side of a mountain, but I couldn't see far enough in any direction to be sure.*

*Then, it was dark, completely dark. Pitch black dark. Now fear began to set in. I froze. My feet were unable to take me anywhere. My chest started to expand and contract rapidly. My throat felt like it was shutting. I couldn't get any air. I felt hot, uncomfortably hot now. Just when I was sure I was about to breathe my last breath, I heard a faint voice.*

*"Find me,"* it echoed.

*I couldn't make it all out, I heard something with an F, but couldn't discern it. I tried to control my breathing so I could hear better.*

*"Find me,"* I hear again.

*Something with "me" I could make out this time. I hoped I could control my breathing once more to hear the whole phrase, whatever it was. I tried to slow my breath.*

*"Find me,"* I heard loud and clear.

*As soon as the words clicked in my head, it was over.*

I sat straight up in the cramped double bed, hitting my forehead on the bunk above me. Ouch.

"Kennedy, you OK?" Nate asked. He must not have been totally asleep, because the movie was still on, and he sounded too alert.

"What? Yeah I'm fine, sorry, did I wake you?" I asked.

"No. Not really, I must have just drifted off for a second; I was still watching the movie. It's almost at the end, your favorite part, where Kit knocks over Dottie at home plate and wins the game," he said excitedly.

Bless his heart, he was still trying to make me happy, and he was right, that was my favorite part. That part and the part where Rosie O'Donnell throws the ball at Dottie's face and she snatches it with her fingers casually. Booyah.

"I can't believe I fell asleep so early, I missed the whole movie," I replied, and now my head was starting to hurt from where I rammed the wooden bunk bed.

"Is your head alright, you hit it pretty hard? What made you jump up?" Nate asked again.

"I'm OK, I might go get some more water and take a Tylenol before I go back to bed. I just had a bad dream, something weird. Do you want anything?" I asked.

"No, I'm OK. But do you want me to come with you?"

"That's alright. I want to get some fresh air too, I'll be back in a minute," I told him.

I walked out into the hallway and was surprised that I didn't hear everyone downstairs. When I got to the bottom of the stairs, I was surprised that the raging games of beer pong weren't going on either. There was a couple all over the couch where Natalie and Kyle had been earlier. There was a guy passed out next to the stone fireplace, and I heard some voices outside.

I grabbed a bottle of water from the fridge, and wandered outside. There was a bonfire going strong that they must have started after I retreated upstairs for the night. It had only been two hours ago, but it seemed like everyone was as tired from the big day as I was. Two boys sat in beach chairs by the fire, smoking cigarettes and had a beer in hand. They asked if I wanted a seat by the fire, and I politely declined. I really didn't even recognize the boys to be honest, but I thought it was nice.

I wondered where Natalie and Kyle had decided to sleep. Once I got a few big gulps of fresh air, I was feeling tired again, and ready for bed. I went back in, climbed the steps, and

walked back into our room. It seemed spacious no\
it would be only Nate and I. I whispered to him,
wanted any water, but he didn't respond. He must
asleep while I was outside. I placed the bottle next t
slid back under the covers, and I was out.

## CHAPTER 5: THE AFTERMATH

"Kennedy? You awake? Kennedy?" I heard Nate asking softly.

I was still kind of groggy. I must not have slept well, but I turned over and sat up.

"Yeah, I'm awake, what time is it?" I asked. My timing was a little off because I had woken up in the middle of the night, banged my head on the bed, and wandered around outside.

"Um, it's like 8:30 a.m. or something. I heard a couple people moving downstairs, it woke me up. You ready to get out of here? I am."

"Oh. Yeah, just give me a minute to brush my hair and teeth and I'll meet you downstairs in, say, five minutes?" I asked him.

"Deal. I'll go find Natalie, and see if Kyle's coming back with us," Nate said.

Nate packed up his little DVD player, and left the room, giving me some privacy. I was thankful, because I'm sure I looked like a hot mess. I am really not a morning person, and my head still hurt a little, to be honest. I grabbed the little duffle bag that Natalie had packed for us, and rummaged through it hoping to find a hairbrush, and some toothpaste. I found the hairbrush, but couldn't find the toothpaste. One for two wasn't bad.

I brushed my hair quickly, and was eager to go downstairs and find Nate and Natalie and get on the road. This party had turned out exactly like I had thought. The people were drunken Neanderthals, Kyle and Natalie had fought, and Nate and I had zero fun, minus watching ten minutes of *A League of Their Own*.

I didn't even make it all the way dowstairs, and Nate yelled up, "Kennedy, I can't find Natalie, can you check the rooms upstairs again?"

Did this mean he had already checked the rooms up here? I wasn't sure, but I turned and went back up the stairs to the first room. I checked each of the remaining three rooms with no luck. There were plenty of sleeping partygoers, but none were Natalie.

"Nate, she's not up here. Did you check everywhere downstairs?" I asked.

"Yeah! Of course I did," Nate yelled back. We got a few hisses from the people passed out all around us. "Shut up," Nate hissed back at them.

I descended the stairs and looked around the rooms downstairs. I couldn't see Natalie or Kyle for that matter. I grabbed Nate's car keys and went to throw the duffle in his car while he kept looking when I spotted Kyle passed out in one of those beach chairs by the remnants of the bonfire last night.

I definitely had not seen him out there when I went on my late night adventure to get some air after I gave myself a concussion. He must have wandered out there and passed out after I had returned to bed.

"Kyle! Wake up! Kyle!" I yelled pretty loudly, but he did not move. "KYLE!" I yelled at the top of my lungs, while nudging his leg with my foot.

"What the hell? What?" Kyle yelled back and braced himself on the chair like a T-Rex was about to attack him.

"Hey, sorry, do you know where Natalie is?" I asked in a lower voice now that I had woken him.

"No. Leave me alone, go back to sleep, it's too early."

"Actually, it's not, but we can't find her and we want to leave," I responded.

"I don't know. She's here somewhere. We'll find a ride back later. You two just go if you want."

"Trust me, I do want to go, but I'm sure Natalie will want to also. Can you just help me look, please?" I asked.

Kyle groaned, obviously displeased that I had ruined his restful slumber, "Now that you woke me up, fine."

I didn't even say thank you, because he was such a piece of work. He walked inside, and I walked around the cabin outside once more, just in case she had a propensity of passing out at random places like her boyfriend apparently did. No luck.

"Kyle, you're such an idiot, how do you not know where your damn girlfriend is?" I heard Nate screaming at Kyle. Now everyone seemed to be waking up in the cabin.

"Shut up, Nate. She wasn't even near me when I passed out last night," Kyle responded while getting in Nate's face.

"Well, where was she then? She didn't come back in our room," Nate said.

"I don't know, we got into another fight, and she stormed away. Didn't see her after that," Kyle said nonchalantly.

"I saw you guys fight," I interjected, "but then I saw you cuddling on the chair like two minutes later."

"Huh? Oh when you stuck your nose in our business? Yeah, we fought again afterwards, she's crazy. I'm done with her," Kyle said. I had never heard him say that. I mean, they fought, but they always made up so quickly that they never really resented each other. He looked like he could care less about her right now, and that was kind of weird to see.

"So you fought again later?" I asked again. "You guys are so pathetic. You're definitely not winning couple of the year that's for sure."

"Whatever, Kennedy, no one asked your opinion, just leave already," Kyle retorted.

I would have left half an hour ago, but we still hadn't found Natalie, and now this was becoming annoying. I picked up my cell phone and dialed Natalie's number. It rang, and rang, and rang, then went to her voicemail.

We all gave the house another once over, and since we made such a ruckus, we were asking everyone else that was still there. It seemed like no one had seen Natalie. I kept trying her cell phone every few minutes, but it just rang until it went to her voicemail, never a voice on the other line. I really had no idea where she could be, but I thought maybe somehow she had called her mom last night, after her fight with Kyle, and maybe her parents came to get her?

I didn't have any other ideas, so I picked up my phone once again and called Natalie's parent's house phone number. On the second ring, I heard a guy's voice outside saying loudly that he remembered seeing Natalie outside last night talking to some random "dude." I hung up and went outside to see what was going on.

"So, you saw her out here last night, by the bonfire, talking to some old guy?" Nate asked.

One of Kyle's deadbeat friends, I think his name is Tanner, looked Nate right in the eye, and seemed very sure about it. "Yeah, man. We were all out here bonging some beers by the fire, and it was Natalie's turn. We saw some guy kinda creeping around, so she went up to him and asked what he was doing here."

I interjected, "So who was this guy, and what did Natalie say to him?"

"I don't know. I heard her calling him a perv or something, and then since she didn't come back, I took her turn and bonged a beer," Tanner said. He seemed to light up whenever he talked about bonging beers, and sounded brain-dead the rest of the time.

Now we knew that Natalie had gone outside to hang out by the bonfire, and confronted some random old guy. Who could that possibly be? Probably someone's dad coming to take them home, I figured.

"So, no one else recognized this guy talking to Natalie?" I posed the question toward Tanner.

Tanner just shrugged his shoulders as if to signal that he was done with this less than exciting conversation. I looked at Nate, and he seemed concerned over this new turn of events. Kyle had wandered away from us while we were talking to Tanner, and I thought that was suspicious. Given the fact that they had fought about a million times last night, and I had walked in on him ready to hit my best friend, I started to get the feeling that he might have done something to her. I really don't want to believe that he really could ever lay a hand on her, let alone hurt her and then lie to us about it, but he was not a stand up person in my eyes. Plus, his girlfriend was basically missing, and he didn't care enough to stand outside with us and try to find her. I thought it all was more than a little shady.

"I'm going to call her cell again, and if she doesn't answer I'm calling her house phone again. Maybe she was upset about the fights and had her mom come get her, I don't know," I repeated my thoughts out loud in case anyone was listening.

"That's a good idea. You make the phone calls, and I'll go through the house, and out back one more time. Be back in a few minutes," Nate responded.

Tanner had wandered inside to probably find more beer, and people were coming outside and loading up in their cars. I yelled, "Hey, listen guys, we can't find Natalie, so if anyone sees her, or hears from her, tell her to call me please!"

"Who are you again?" I heard from someone jumping in the back of a black Escalade. The question was followed by condescending laughing, and then the sound of doors slamming.

If I wasn't so worried about finding Natalie, that remark might have bothered me a lot more, but in my present state of mind, I could care less. I dialed Natalie's cell one more time, and got the same response, nothing. I redialed her mom's house phone, and this time let it ring beyond two rings. Natalie's mom answered on the fourth ring.

"Hello?" she asked.

"Hi, Mrs. Hall, it's Kennedy," I responded.

"Oh, hi dear, how are you? Are you guys on your way home?" she continued.

"Um, not exactly. So, Natalie's not with you I'm guessing?" I asked.

"With me? No, of course not. What are you talking about? Is this a joke? It's not funny," Mrs. Hall shrieked, I could hear her heart racing through the phone. She was worried. Now I was worried.

"No, I'm sorry. I don't know what to do now, Mrs. Hall."

"Natalie's really not with you? Put her on the phone right now, this is not funny!" she screamed.

"No, I'm sorry. No, this isn't a prank or a joke, and I'm really worried now too. We have checked every room in the house five times, we've asked everyone at the party, and we've checked outside all around the house. We can't find her. I'm sorry," I said.

"Kennedy," she started with tears in her voice, "if you are not kidding me, and you all really can't find Natalie," she paused, "then you need to call the police immediately, and Mr. Hall will be on our way. What is the address to this cabin place again? Oh wait, I have it here, nevermind."

"OK, I'll call them right now," I said, and hung up before I could hear her response, if there was any.

Nate was right next to me, and had heard the entire conversation with Mrs. Hall. While he was dialing 9-1-1 on his phone, I called my mom to fill her in. The conversation went much like it did with Natalie's mother. My mom also said she was on her way, even though I told her I was with Nate and was fine.

Nate said the police were initially hesitant because we were high school kids and thought we may be playing a prank, but after he convinced them that we were not kidding they said they were sending a few squad cars up to speak with us. Most of the kids had started to leave by this point anyhow, and once they heard the cops were coming, they left even faster. I guess they didn't want the cops to cite them for underage drinking, or whatever else they were doing. I tried to get people to stay--- the cops said no one should leave--- but no one listened to me.

The police arrived and immediately stopped anyone else from leaving. At this point, only Nate, myself, Kyle, Dax, Tanner, and two more boys were there. They went to Dax first, since he was responsible for the house. I don't know what they asked him, but it only took a minute or two. I'm sure they got zero information out of him. They then went to Nate since he was the one who made the call. I was standing next to Nate, and the officer wanted to speak to both of us to get all of the information we had. We recounted the story of when we last saw Natalie, and how we woke up this morning and couldn't find her anywhere. I told the officer I had already called her parents and they were on their way. He asked me if I had tried her cell phone, and I told him I had numerous times, but it rang and then went to voicemail.

He asked us the standard questions of if we saw anything unusual, and if she had any fights last night. With Kyle staring at me, I told him how Kyle was Natalie's boyfriend, and that they did, in fact, have a few fights last night but that it was normal behavior for them. The officer chomped on his gum, closed his notepad, and turned to glare at Kyle. He then went and took Kyle aside, and led him into the house. Nate and I were left outside with the rest of the remaining people. My mom had called me while I was talking to the officer, so I called her back. She was still worried, and asked if the police had shown up. I told her that there was an officer here, and nothing had changed, and if it did that I would call her immediately.

Just out of habit, I dialed Natalie's number once more, hoping somehow she would answer it this time, and that this was all a big mix up. It rang once, then twice, then a third time, and this time I heard her answer!

"Natalie! Natalie, where are you?" I excitedly yelled.

"This is not Natalie, this is Officer Monroe," the voice on the other line smoothly replied.

"What? Wait, what?" I was totally confused.

"Who is this?" the voice asked, and just then, I saw the officer walk out of the house holding Natalie's phone, talking to me.

"Oh, I'm sorry," I said to the officer. "I just kept trying to call her. Where did you find that?" I asked.

"Inside the house. We heard it ringing. I picked it up by the microwave," he told me.

I must have seen her phone earlier today, but there were twenty cell phones lying around all over the house. I don't know how I couldn't have heard it when we called all those times earlier. Too much commotion going on, I guess. So, her cell phone was still here, but she obviously wasn't.

This was the first time I really let my mind wander as to what could have happened to my friend. She might be somewhere without a phone, with no way to contact anyone for help. She must be so scared, I knew I was.

The questioning continued with the officer asking us if we thought there was any possibility that Natalie just went to visit another friend, or if Natalie ran away because of her fight with Kyle. We told him that we didn't know anyone else in Deep Creek and just came here for the after party, and that no, we didn't think she would run away without telling us, and she definitely wouldn't have left her cell phone here. Eventually Mr. and Mrs. Hall arrived. They must have been absolutely flying down the road to get here so quickly.

They ran up to the police, and the officer who was first here, Officer Monroe, tried to calm her mom down as best he could. He must have explained the situation to them, and then took them inside. Mrs. Hall came outside to talk to me a little later, and wanted me to explain everything I knew in detail. I told her about the fight with Kyle, how he had raised his hand to Natalie, but then that they had made up. I told her that she never came to our room though, and how Kyle had said they had another fight. I then told her about the weird older man who was outside. Wait, how did I forget to tell the police this? I ran away from Mrs. Hall.

"Officer Monroe! Officer Monroe!" I yelled as I ran inside the cabin. "Officer Monroe, I forgot to tell you something," I didn't take a breath as I kept rattling on, "There was a guy. An older man or something. Tanner told us earlier today. People were outside at the bonfire and some older guy came up, and Natalie walked over to him, and Tanner heard her call him a weirdo, or a perv, or a creeper, something like that."

"An older man?" he asked, probably confused by my word jumble.

"Yes, I guess. I was asleep, I don't know. Ask Tanner, he told us this morning, that some older guy was there. I thought it might have been someone's dad picking them up so I kind of just forgot about it until now."

"Well, was it someone's father?" he asked.

"I don't know," I answered earnestly.

"Well, it probably was someone's dad, so it's not really pertinent here, but I'll mark it down. What's your name again, dear?" Even the cop couldn't remember my name. Awesome.

"Kennedy," I replied, holding back the tears. "Kennedy Clark."

# CHAPTER 6:

# THE INQUISITION CONTINUES

It's 11 p.m., and my mom and I are finally pulling into our neighborhood, with Nate and his parents following behind us. Nate only lives a few houses down from mine on the same street. The cops didn't keep us at Dax's cabin that long after they questioned us, but we all stayed and drove around with the Hall's. We must have been up and down almost every street in that small lake town. I don't know what we were hoping for, it's not like Natalie would have just been walking around on the side of the road for us to pick her up. Nevertheless, we searched for hours until almost 8 at night, and then we headed home.

My eyes were puffy and hurt from all the crying I did on the way home. I tried to keep it together, but every time I saw Mrs. Hall break down, I started crying again, which then made my mom start crying, and it was a big mess. I really have no idea how we got to this point. This was supposed to be an epic night, Natalie promised. Now she was god knows where with god knows who.

I thought the cops were really keying in on Kyle. I guess that is normal since he is the boyfriend. As Kyle was getting into his parent's SUV, I heard Officer Monroe, the first cop on the scene, bark at him not to leave Pittsburgh once he got home. I guess this was a threatening gesture, but Kyle didn't seem concerned. He still had that same dumb look on his face as he always did.

My mom must have known I was upset and she graciously didn't run me through the twenty questions game on our way home. We stopped with Nate's family at a little diner to get some food, but quickly realized no one was hungry, so we got back on the road. As everything grew silent, driving on those dark, windy, mountain roads, I started to cry, and I let it all out. My mom just let me cry, and held my hand.

When we were finally in our driveway, I wasn't even sure if I had enough strength to get out of the car and into my house. I had never felt this way before. I am by no means a drama queen, and I certainly wasn't in the habit of crying and letting my mother hold my hand, but something had taken over me, and my legs felt like lead.

My mom got out of the driver's seat and looked through the windshield at me, motionless. "Are you OK, Kennedy?" she asked.

I just looked at her with my eyelids fighting to stay open.

"Kennedy?" she questioned once more. She walked over to my side of the car, opened the door, and put her hand out to let me use it as a crutch. I still couldn't move. I saw her, I saw what she was doing, I wanted to respond, but I couldn't do anything.

"Kennedy, honey, do you need a lift? Here ya go," she said as she sort of bent toward me and tried to grab the back of my sweatshirt and haul me up. She was partially successful, and I guess my body just needed a little help. I found my footing and was able to stand with a little help from my mom.

I found my voice but, "Sorry, Mom," was all I could muster.

"It's OK, honey, you've had a long day. Let's just get you inside and let you rest, OK?"

I walked in through the garage and into the kitchen. My mom asked if I wanted any hot tea. I shrugged, and kept on walking toward the stairs.

"Honey, do you need any help getting up to your room?" she asked. She must be worried, I hadn't heard her say "honey" this many times in years.

"No, I'm fine."

"OK, I'll be right up. I'm going to make us some tea, it will help us sleep," she said. My mom tended to do this, though--- she inserted "us" when she really meant "I"--- somehow always lumping me into the same category as her. I learned a long time ago, probably when I was about eight and corrected everyone for everything, not to bother to correct my mom on her pronoun usage.

I kept trudging upstairs, and each step felt like it would be the last I could absolutely bear. My bedroom door was open, and I somehow flew into my bed, face down on the pillows. I let my body rest, and soon heard my mom come in with the tea.

I was now on my back and holding a cup of fresh tea with honey and could see my mom's lips moving but couldn't really hear her. I was so exhausted, and my mind wandered back to the cabin, to what the police were doing now. Were Mr. and

Mrs. Hall still driving the roads of Deep Creek, Maryland, hoping to find their daughter? Was the yellow crime scene tape still wrapped around the cabin?

My mom's lips kept moving for what seemed like days but must have only been minutes. She took my tea from me, placed it on my nightstand, pulled my comforter up over me, and shut off my light as she exited my room. I have no idea what she said, but I was thankful she left. I needed to stare into the blackness of my room, let it envelop me, and let it drain the sadness and pain I had in me right now because my best friend was missing. I was staring at my ceiling, now very glad that I had it painted a deep purple, and not a standard white. The brightness would have hurt my eyes at a time like this.

I thought about everything, and I thought about nothing. Then, all of a sudden, my mom burst into my room with a fresh glass of tea in hand and a bowl of cereal. My mom had officially gone crazy. What was she doing back in my room so soon? I thought she wanted to let me rest.

"Good morning, honey. Oh, you're up, how are you?" she asked.

Good morning? What? "What do you mean good morning?" I mumbled.

"It's morning, dear. It's 9 a.m. How did you sleep?" she replied. I think once she opened my curtains, and could see my face and eyes, she could see that I hadn't slept a single minute.

"Oh, Kennedy. Tell me you fell asleep? Were you scared? You could have come to get me, honey."

How could it be 9 a.m. already? It felt like a few minutes, half an hour, tops.

"Do you want me to shut the blinds and let you get some sleep now? Oh, I'll have to call the police and tell them that you'll go by the station a little later today. But that's OK, that'll be no problem," my mother said.

"What about the cops? Did they find Natalie? Why am I going to the station? Am I in trouble? Is Natalie ok?" I ran off all these questions so fast.

"No, they haven't found her yet, and no you are not in trouble. They wanted you to come by so they could ask you some more questions."

"The cops from Deep Creek?" I was confused.

"No, honey, the cops from here; the local ones. I guess the police in Deep Creek had connected with the police here. They are working together so they can find Natalie quickly."

My mind raced to that show on one of those crazy stations on TV, called *48 Hours*. They always say that the most important time is the first 48 hours after a crime is committed. I think usually the show is about murders, but, wait, no, Natalie wasn't murdered. I had never thought about that possibility. I thought hurt, maybe. I thought maybe she ran away because she was so upset with Kyle. I never thought murdered. Oh my God, was my best friend dead? My heart started racing, and I felt lightheaded. I flopped back down on my back, and turned on my side and covered my face with a pillow. I wished this were a dream.

"I'm going to call the police and tell them you'll be down later, you try to shut your eyes and get some rest. Drink some tea, that will help," my mom was pushing the tea on me again.

"I don't want any god damn tea, Mom!" I snapped back.

"OK. Calm down, honey," my mom said as she quickly made her way out of my room.

I still felt the energy surge through my body, and I got up and walked into the hallway. My mom was on the phone with who I hoped was the police. I walked downstairs and into the garage. My mom asked what I was doing, and I told her I was going to the police station. My mom tried to persuade me to stay, but once she knew the battle was lost, she quickly hopped into the passenger side of the car. I probably should not have been driving, but I was thinking in the here and now, not about the what ifs or consequences.

The police station seemed empty, even for a Sunday morning. There was barely anybody working it looked like, and the receptionist seemed confused as to what I was talking about when I said Natalie's name. What kind of operation were they running here anyhow? The receptionist finally clued in on what was going on, and she lead me to a desk nearby. Officer Something was sitting there, feet on his desk, drinking coffee and perusing a file of some sort. What the hell?

"Excuse me," I snapped.

"Excuse you," he replied. "What can I do for you?"

"I'm Kennedy Clark, I'm here about Natalie Hall's disappearance."

"Oh, yeah, take a seat. So, we wanted to go over some things with you, if that's OK," he asked.

"Yeah, that's fine, but I told the cops in Deep Creek every little detail, didn't they give you the information? Aren't you working on this together?" I demanded.

"Listen, sweetie, let me do my job, and I'll find your friend, OK?" he said condescendingly. I hate, hate, hate when people call me sweetie, only my mom gets away with it, but certainly not men, and certainly not this arrogant man.

"Well, if you'd do your job instead of kicking your feet up, I'd feel more confident and not have to ask so many questions," I came back at him.

My mom pinched my elbow in embarrassment, I'm sure, and the cop just took a big gulp of his coffee and pretended he didn't hear my last sentence. He went through the entire night with me, every little detail. I was growing more and more annoyed because I felt like we were wasting time. The cops in Deep Creek literally could have copied their notes and emailed them to these guys, and we could have cut out all this useless junk.

After I recounted every detail, he asked me about Kyle and Natalie's relationship. He asked me about every fight they've had, and I told him that they fought every day so it was impossible to recount every fight. He kind of got the picture after I said that. He asked me if Kyle was violent, and I answered honestly, "No." I did tell him that Kyle had a raised hand toward her, but as far as I knew, and I know Natalie told me everything, Kyle had never touched her like that. He asked me if Kyle was a jealous boyfriend, I answered honestly again, "Yes." He asked if Natalie had ever cheated on Kyle, "No." He asked if there was a chance Natalie was pregnant, "No." He asked if Natalie had every complained about her parents, "Yes, like every normal teenager." He asked if she ever complained that she wanted to run away, "No, nothing like that." He asked if Natalie ever dated an older man, "No." Why was he asking these weird questions? He made it seem like Natalie was a ditzy, ungrateful, teenage slut, which she most certainly was not. She may have not had the best judgment in Kyle, but she was none of the above.

After a string of unproductive answers by me, the cop asked if I saw the man that Natalie was talking to. I told him that I had not, and that I only learned of this man's presence from Tanner, Kyle's friend. He kind of smirked at my answer.

"Why are you smirking? What?" I asked defensively.

"No reason," he responded.

"No, there definitely was a reason. You haven't even moved your face in half an hour, now all of a sudden you smirk."

"You're pretty observant," the cop noticed.

"So?" I questioned.

"Well, it just seems unlikely that a random older man came to the party and spoke to your friend, that's all. Forget it, kid. Let's move on. How well do you know these guys, Kyle, Tanner, Dax?" he asked.

I told him that I knew Kyle the best, only because of Natalie, and although I disliked him, he was harmless, or so I thought. I had never spoken to Dax, and knew of Tanner from growing up in the same school, but never really talked to him.

"How were you at a party with all them then?" he questioned.

"Only because of Natalie, trust me," I responded.

Officer Whatever asked me more questions that were super mundane, then said I could go. I wanted to get away from him, but I felt like nothing was getting done. I wondered how everything was going in Deep Creek.

"So, do you guys have any leads at all?" I asked, as my mom was trying to usher me out the front of the police station.

"We've got this, kid," was all he said. With that, I turned in disgust and stormed out of the station like a 3-year-old having a tantrum.

My mom tried to get me to sleep when we got back home, but I was too wired. I felt like I had to do something. I felt helpless. I walked into the house, and straight up to my room, shutting the door behind me. My mom didn't even try to come in. I saw that I had left so quickly this morning that I forgot my phone was charging on my nightstand next to my bed. Nine missed calls. My heart beat quickly, could one of those be from Natalie? Probably not, but I was excited that maybe it could be. I scanned my missed call list. Eight calls from Nate, and one from Kyle. Why was Kyle calling me? How did I have Kyle's number programmed into my phone? Then, I remembered, Natalie had programmed it in just in case her phone ever died, she said she could use my phone to call him. Great. Natalie was always messing with my phone. I decided to call Nate back first.

He just wanted to see how I was doing, if I had slept at all, because he had trouble. I told him I didn't sleep at all, but that I wasn't really tired. I told him about the police, and he said he was supposed to go there in a few minutes to talk to them. I warned him about Officer Knows Nothing. My conversation with Nate went much better than the ones I had been having with my mom. I told him to call me after his interview with the cops, and he agreed.

I was sitting Indian-style in my bed now, staring all around, focusing on nothing in particular, and nothing for longer than a second. I almost felt like my body was not my own. I didn't really have control on where my eyes were looking or where my head was turning, but the rest of my body was perfectly still. I don't know how long I was in this position, but my phone rang again, and I thought it would be Nate, thinking it was a fast meeting with the cops, but it wasn't, it was my father.

Jack Clark is my father. He doesn't live with us though. He lives down in one of those areas near Washington D.C. My mom and dad divorced when I was four, and my dad moved there right after. We are still on good terms, and I talk to my dad like any other teenage girl talks to their dad, fleetingly, but we're certainly not a family. He has his own family in D.C. now. My dad remarried a few years after he divorced my mom. Janet is his new wife, and she has two kids of her own she brought into their makeshift family. My dad, bless his heart, always tries to make me feel comfortable and welcome down with his new family, but the truth is, there is no room for me, and I could never leave my mom alone, so living there is out of the question completely.

I reluctantly answered the phone, "Yes, Dad."

"Kennedy, are you OK? Your mother just called me and told me about Natalie. Are you OK? I'm driving up right now. I'm coming," he rattled on.

"Dad, I'm fine. Mom worries, you know her. Don't come up here, I'm fine, really," I tried to reassure my father that I was OK, when I obviously was not.

"Are you sure? I can be there in a few hours. How are you feeling? Your mother said you didn't sleep at all last night, is this true? God, Kennedy, you need sleep."

"Dad. Dad. Woah, slow down. I slept a little," I lied, "Mom's being dramatic. I'm really OK, but I have to go make some calls. I love you, bye," and with that, I hung up the phone. Now, if that was my mother she would have called right back before I could even dial another number, but for my dad, that was enough. The conversation was over, and I was sure he wasn't on his way here.

I figured it was time to call Kyle back. I called and he answered on the first ring.

"What the hell, Kennedy, what did you tell those cops?" he said angrily.

"What? Kyle, I didn't tell them anything that was untrue, I actually stuck up for you saying you were pretty harmless," I replied back.

"Harmless? Right. You lying bitch, I know you told them I hit her, or abused her, or something; they are all over my ass right now. They questioned me this morning, and they want me to come back in later today. What did you say, you jealous bitch?" he yelled.

"Hey asshole, I didn't say anything bad, although now I'm thinking I should have, you insane, psychotic, maniac! I told them the truth, I never said you hit her or did any of that," I yelled back at him. I saw my mom peep her head in through my door, but I waived her off. I started to think, why exactly is he getting so upset, if he didn't do anything, why is he so worried? If he didn't do anything, then just tell the cops the honest truth, and hope that it helps them find Natalie. Maybe he had more to hide than I thought.

The other end of the phone was silent. "Did you tell the cops everything you knew?" I asked. No response. "Kyle, did you tell them everything you knew from last night, everything you remember?" Still no response. "Kyle!" I yelled, and I heard a crunching noise, like something had fallen, and then a deep voice, "Kyle, get off the phone right now! Stop screwing around," and then I heard Kyle respond to the other voice.

"Dad, I'm not screwing around. It's Kennedy on the phone and I'm setting her straight so she stops telling the cops lies," Kyle responded to his dad. Then I heard a click, and Kyle was gone.

# CHAPTER 7: GUT FEELING

Kyle's dad had lost it. He couldn't handle Natalie missing and all of the attention that it was bringing to his son. He heard his son screaming on the phone at me, and he just lost it. The click I had heard was the aftermath of Kyle's dad throwing him down on the ground and then hanging up the phone. I now understood where Kyle got his violent temper from. I only learned all of this information from my mom who heard it from Mrs. Hall. Luckily, a cop had been passing through the neighborhood and heard yelling and things breaking from inside Kyle's house. Curious timing, but at least they were useful. The cop apparently knocked on the door and eventually burst through and peeled Kyle's dad off of him to stop the fight.

A few minutes after my phone call with Kyle, that ended extremely abruptly, an officer I had never seen before showed up at my front door. He asked me the same questions for the fifteenth time about Natalie and Kyle's relationship, and if, in my opinion, I thought Kyle had done something to Natalie. I responded that no I did not think Kyle actually hurt her, or did anything else to her either. I'm not sure why I was so sure that Kyle had nothing to do with Natalie's disappearance, and Lord knows I totally dislike the kid, but I just had a gut feeling that he had no part in this.

The officer was only at my house for a few minutes, and after I had repeated myself a million times, he left. As soon as he walked out of the door, my mind was wandering again as to what I could do to help the situation. Now that my gut was sure Kyle was innocent in this ordeal, there was still something missing in this puzzle, and it seemed like the police still had no idea where to start. How many times could they ask me and Kyle questions?

A lightning bolt idea hit my mind, and I swore I even heard a voice telling me to go back to Deep Creek. I should have been tired from my nonexistent sleep last night, but this was a logical idea, or so I thought. I grabbed my cell to call Nate, and see if he'd come with me, when my mom scurried back into the living room.

"Honey, I made you an appointment in twenty minutes, I'll go with you," she said.

"Appointment for what?" I asked, irritated that she was already foiling my plans to venture back to the scene of the crime.

"With Dr. Sadler, she's a psychiatrist, honey."

"What are you talking about? I'm not going anywhere, especially to some psychiatrist!" I protested. I had no idea what my mom was thinking right now.

"Kennedy, she's a friend of a friend, and she's coming in on a Sunday just for you, because I'm worried about you, honey. I can see it in your eyes and face, you are reeling over Natalie, and you haven't slept a wink, and maybe she can give you something to help you rest, or calm down. I don't know, I'm not a doctor, but you are going, and I'll go with you."

"Mom, I am not going. I want to go back to Dax's cabin in Deep Creek, with Nate. I have a feeling we could figure something out, maybe help the police," I replied, knowing this wouldn't help my case.

"Kennedy, this is exactly what I'm talking about. You are not a detective; please let them deal with this and stay out of their way. You already gave that nice police officer so much attitude this morning. You need to concentrate on getting some rest right now, and taking care of yourself. I'm worried."

First of all, that was not a lot of attitude, and that lazy ass cop deserved it, but there was no use arguing with her, so I did what I did best and cut a deal. "Mom, OK, how about I go to this appointment, see this doctor, and then afterward you let me and Nate drive back down to Deep Creek for an hour, that's it, then we'll come back. Can we do that?" I pleaded. I could suffer through an hour or so with this shrink, then jet down to Deep Creek and see if we can figure anything out.

"Kennedy, no, that is not going to happen. And, honey, it's already afternoon, by the time we are done with Dr. Sadler, and you get down to Deep Creek it would be dark anyhow, so no, that's not a deal," she responded. It wasn't like my mom to be this forceful. I could see she meant business.

"OK, how about I go see Dr. Sadler today, with you, and then maybe tomorrow, first thing in the morning, you let me go back to Deep Creek?" I asked, knowing full well I was not waiting until tomorrow to go. This would just make her think she had more time to convince me not to go.

"That sounds reasonable, I suppose. Well, we better get going, we don't want to be late for Dr. Sadler," she announced, and started toward the garage door.

I followed dutifully, thinking how bad could one hour with a psychiatrist be?

Well, it was pretty bad, let me tell you that. Dr. Sadler was nice and all, but I could tell the entire time that she was talking down to me. My mother must have told her some crazy stuff. She was treating me like a child, not an 18-year-old who just found out her best friend had disappeared out of thin air. She asked me if I had been having any strange dreams, and at first I told her "No," but I finally told her about the dream I had two nights ago, the night Natalie disappeared. I thought maybe she could tell me why I had that dream, if it was connected to Natalie's disappearance, or just a random dream, but she just nodded her head and scribbled on her notepad in her lap. This clearly was not going to help me at all. She asked me if I had gotten any sleep since Friday night, and I told her that I hadn't, but I felt fine, except that my head hurt a little, but that was probably from hitting it on that stupid bunk bed Friday night at the cabin. Again, she nodded and scribbled something down.

A painful hour passed and she called my mother in. She asked if it was OK if she spoke in front of my mother, since I was eighteen, she legally couldn't unless I gave permission. I didn't think it was a big deal so I said it was fine. She said that she believed I was suffering from the early onset of Post Traumatic Stress Disorder (PTSD). Even though the event was very new, and still going on, it was a tragic and startling event in my young life. She said it wasn't uncommon for someone to experience PTSD after going through something like this.

I wanted to hear none of it, and interjected that this was a bunch of bologna and I was fine, but my mom shooshed me like only she knows how. She told me she was going to prescribe me a daily medication, Paxil, which would help me with the

PTSD. It would help me stay calm, and not become overwhelmed thinking of what has happened with Natalie. She also suggested a sleep aid. She said she understood it must be difficult for me to rest my mind and try to sleep at a time like this, but that I really needed to for my health and sanity. I'd had enough of her mumbo jumbo, and I knew I was never going to take either of those medications she told my mom to pick up for me. I just nodded my head, and my mom must have thought I was finally succumbing to her rationale. I really just needed to get out of this office, call Nate, and get on the road back to Deep Creek.

My mother seemed happy, like she was saving me or something. She was being so dramatic. One sleepless night was not a big deal, and most teenagers my age did that on a weekly basis, for fun. I didn't understand why Nadene was so worried. I didn't have time to think about it though, because as soon as we were in the car, I texted Nate and told him I was going back to Deep Creek, and I'd pick him up in ten. He quickly responded and said he was in. I could always count on Nate.

As soon as my mom and I got back to the house, I told her that I would run down to the pharmacy and pick up the prescriptions that Dr. Sadler prescribed for me. She smiled, apparently very pleased at my acceptance that I needed help. She handed over the keys, and I was off.

Nate and I made it back to Deep Creek in what seemed like no time at all. I shouldn't have been going as fast as I was, but I was rehashing the last twelve hours, and how my mom was insane, and we were trying to formulate a game plan as to what exactly we were going to do when we got back there. By the time we pulled up to Dax's cabin, it was about 5 p.m. Sunday night. It had been anywhere from 33 to 39 hours since Natalie's disappearance. Since we really still had no idea when she disappeared, I figured 2 a.m. was about the last time anyone really remembered seeing her. We were quickly approaching that precious 48-hour mark when most cases are solved, or the reality that they may never be solved starts to set in.

It was still light out, but the shade of the trees made it seem later than it actually was. One thing we hadn't planned on was the door being locked because no one was home. So we were standing outside of Dax's cabin, with no way to get in, and nowhere really to look except for the yellow crime scene tape that was still affixed around the house and driveway. Since there was nowhere else to go, I started to walk up the hill toward the woods, and Nate followed.

"So what are we going to do?" he asked.

"I'm not sure, but for some reason I want to look in the woods a little," I replied. I had no idea what I was looking for, but my gut was telling me to walk around a bit.

"What are we looking for?" Nate asked, with a hint of annoyance in his voice.

"Nate, I'm not sure. If you want to wait here, that's fine, I'll just be a minute."

"No, no, I'm coming, calm down."

I continued walking through the woods on the side of the mountain. They weren't heavily wooded. There were tons of trees, but still enough space in between so that you could see a good ways ahead and on each side of you. It was cluttered with large rocks; you could probably even classify them as boulders. Some of the rocks were as tall as I was, and maybe ten feet long. They were beautiful, and I could see how this would be an awesome place to just sit and think without any disruptions. I walked up the inclined side of the mountain for a minute, but then I felt like someone had grabbed my arm and was pulling me sideways. I tripped a little, and Nate asked if I was OK. I tried to describe the feeling I just felt, but he was skeptical of my explanation. So was I, but I definitely felt like someone was grabbing me and pulling me in this direction.

I followed in the direction I was pulled toward, and about 30 yards to the left, I saw another big boulder in front of me.

"Now what?" Nate asked.

"I don't feel the pulling anymore," I told him.

He kind of snorted a little, which he always did when he didn't believe something, but I didn't care. For some reason, I was pulled to this exact spot. We weren't far from our original starting place, and we were only a few yards from the car, which we could easily see through the spaces in the trees we were standing among.

"Something is here, I feel it," I told him.

"Kennedy, you are kind of acting weird. Are you all of a sudden a psychic or something? You're freaking me out, like you've lost it."

I didn't pay any attention to Nate's comments because I was so sure that I was being drawn to this exact spot. I wasn't psychic, I didn't think, but we all have gut feelings. If I didn't follow my gut on this, and Natalie is never found, I could never live with myself just thinking that I might have possibly been able to help.

I continued to stare at this boulder, and then all of a sudden my eyes darted down to the corner of the boulder where it met the ground. I followed the dirt line around to the back of the rock, and I thought I saw something shiny. I squatted down and used a twig to touch something that looked like silver. I didn't want to get my hands dirty, and I thought if it was possibly evidence, I didn't want my fingerprints on it. I don't know how

I thought of this so quickly, but I did. Nate was now interested as he saw me studying something on the ground.

"What do you see? What is that?" he asked as his eyes narrowed down to the object.

"It looks like something silver. Can you find me a thicker stick, this one keeps snapping," I asked. A second later Nate handed me a thicker stick, and I was pushing the leaves and dirt aside to get to whatever it was we saw.

I gasped. "What is it?" Nate asked, his voice getting a little higher.

"I think...I think it is Natalie's Tiffany's bracelet," I replied back. I kept using the stick to dig around the middle of the bracelet until it was completely visible. The oval middle was engraved with the letters PSU. Natalie's parents had been so excited that she chose to go to their alma mater that her mom ran out and bought her this Tiffany's bracelet and had PSU engraved on it. I used the stick to flip the oval over, because I knew that under the PSU was Natalie's initials, and there they were, NH for Natalie Hall.

I stumbled backward, tripped over something on the ground and landed right on my butt. Nate didn't even react to my fall; he was still staring right at the bracelet next to the rock. My mind raced to what we should do next. Who do we call? Should I call and tell my mom? Do we call the police down here, or the police back in Pittsburgh? I don't even know their numbers. Would 9-1-1 do? I really had no idea. Nate must have noticed I was on the ground and he looked over to me.

"What now?" he asked the same question I had been thinking as well.

"I don't know. How could the police have missed this?" I asked.

"I don't know, Kennedy. It was buried a little bit, I don't know, just what do we do now?" he asked again, reaching into his pocket for his cell.

"We left our phones in the car, remember?" I told him.

"Oh yeah, I'm going to get mine, and figure out who we should call, I'll be right back," he said. Nate walked the short walk back to my car to retrieve his cell, and I got back up on my feet and approached the rock and bracelet again. I squatted down again, but this time I just grabbed the bracelet with my two hands. I didn't care about fingerprints anymore. The police are stupid for not finding this, and I could not believe what I was seeing. This presented a whole different set of scenarios in my mind as to Natalie's disappearance. Why was her bracelet on the ground wedged under the rock? Was she that drunk that she walked through the woods, hit her bracelet off the rocks, and it fell here? Did she get into a physical fight with someone and that's how it got knocked off? Things were not looking good, and my mind wandered to a place where Natalie was hurt and scared and no one was even close to finding her. I started to cry a little without even realizing it and then I heard Nate. "What the heck? Put that down, Kennedy! I thought you weren't going to hold it! Geez!" Nate exploded.

"I had to. I can't believe this, Nate she is hurt, I know it. Someone took her, she didn't run away, I know it now," I managed to blurt out.

"I'm calling 9-1-1. I'll try to get a cop up here, put the bracelet down!" Nate snapped.

Within minutes, and much faster than the first time we called 9-1-1 in Deep Creek, there were two cop cars tearing into Dax's driveway. We were standing by my car when they pulled up.

Officer Monroe was one of the officers, and he recognized us right away. It had not even been two days since we were standing here talking to him the first time. We showed him back into the woods where the rock was. I had placed Natalie's bracelet on top of the rock. I told him how I touched it, and he made a face as to tell me I shouldn't have, but I told him I couldn't help it. They carefully placed it in an evidence bag, and then the barrage of questions came.

Why were we here? How did we know the bracelet was by the rock? How do we know it was Natalie's? Did we put this here? Why were we trespassing? Does Dax know we are here? Do our parents know that we are here? Officer Monroe tried to calm down some of the other officers when they were bombarding us with questions, but we tried to stay calm and answer them all. We came because we had a hunch we might be able to help, nothing more. We didn't know the bracelet was there, we were shocked to find it; we were just looking. We didn't put the bracelet there. We weren't aware we were trespassing; we were just trying to help. Dax doesn't know we are here. Our parents don't know either. Then, one police officer glared at me and said that I must have put it there because they had officers searching this entire area for hours and never found it. It would have been impossible for them not to spot it. I looked him straight in the eye because I was going to tell him that obviously they weren't competent in their jobs if I found it in five minutes and they couldn't, but I held my tongue. I told him that I was just looking around and I felt like I was drawn to this area. At this, he laughed. A few other officers chuckled as well, but not Officer Monroe.

Officer Monroe did his best to shield us from the other officer's comments because they were not guarding what came out of their mouths at this point. After being questioned for another fifteen minutes, Officer Monroe took us aside. He told us that we were trespassing, and since this is an active crime scene that we were really jeopardizing Natalie's investigation by being here and tampering with the area. I didn't consider finding a piece of Natalie's bracelet tampering with the area, but the cops were telling us to leave and not to come back to Dax's cabin. There wasn't much Nate and I could do, but just by finding Natalie's bracelet under the rock, I felt empowered. I thought this was solid proof that Natalie didn't just run off somewhere by herself. She was definitely taken by someone. We had no idea by who just yet, but I felt I could still help. Maybe my dreams were trying to help me. Who knows? I did get that feeling like someone was pulling me to that exact area where we found the bracelet. I decided I'm going to listen to my gut from now on. If my gut told me to drive back to Deep Creek tomorrow, I would. If my gut told me to call someone I thought might know something, I would. I was going to do anything and everything I could to find Natalie, because I was sure now more than ever that she needed someone's help.

I guess Nate and I were lucky, because after we promised to stay out of the police's way, Officer Monroe convinced his colleagues to let us leave without any further repercussions. Unfortunately, we weren't totally saved of the wrath that our parents put on us for our excursion back to Deep Creek once we got back home.

As soon as Nate and I settled into the car, we checked our phones and saw that each of us had plenty of missed calls, all coming from our parents. I had twelve from my mom, and three from my dad. Nate had comparable calls on his phone as well. I made a quick call to my mother, telling her we were on our way home from Deep Creek, we were fine, and we'd be home before she knew it. My mom was screaming back at me in the phone, but I just pulled it away from my ear for a moment, and then told her I loved her and would be home soon. Easy enough. Nate wasn't as lucky. His mom ripped into him for a full five minutes, and I could hear her from my seat. She also forbid him from ever talking to me again, to which he replied that she was unrealistic, but she kept on her rant.

After our exhausting calls to the parents, Nate and I barely spoke on the dark ride home. I should have been exhausted seeing as I had been up for an ungodly amount of hours, and Nate kept asking me if I wanted him to take over driving, but I felt fine. Well, fine wasn't really the word, but rather than feeling tired, I felt invigorated. I thought I had the key, somehow, to figure out where Natalie was. I was optimistic. Nate was not. He kept his thoughts to himself until we pulled into our neighborhood. I started to slow the car as we approached his house, and he turned in his seat to look at me.

"Kennedy, do you think she's still alive?" he asked, softly, almost afraid to say it loud as if his worst fears would somehow be realized by speaking it.

"Of course I do!" I scoffed back. How could he believe for one second that she would not still be alive? I didn't understand.

"Well, I mean, I hope that she is. I don't even pray, but I will pray tonight that she is. It's just, the bracelet in the woods--- it seems like someone maybe…" and his voice trailed off.

"I know. It seems like someone grabbed her, or maybe got into a fight with her, right? I was thinking that too, and that is really scary. I still have no idea who that person would be, but I just got this feeling today," I started to explain.

"That feeling like someone was pulling you to that spot, you told me. What do you think that's about?" he asked.

"No, I was going to say, I had a feeling that she is alive, and needs my, or our, help. I don't know what that pulling feeling was, but it worked, it led me right to the bracelet. I think I have to follow these feelings, so far it's helped," I told him. I could tell Nate was hesitant to believe my theories of my gut being able to lead us to Natalie eventually, but he couldn't argue with the fact that it led me right to the bracelet. I actually don't even care, I know what I feel, and that's all I can go on right now.

I pulled up to his driveway, and let Nate out. I could see his mother peering through the front window. I swear, that lady has a stare like Medusa, one good look and you're stone. Nate got out of the car, and turned as he shut the door.

"Night, Kennedy," Nate said sadly.

"Goodnight, Nate. I'll text you later," I replied back, trying to cheer up the mood he was currently in.

I watched Nate walk away and had this empty feeling in my stomach. I couldn't really tell if it was because I was hungry, since we hadn't eaten since this morning, or because there was a feeling Nate wasn't really on the same track as me. We weren't thinking alike, and I could tell he was skeptical about my gut feeling theory.

When I arrived home, my mother was waiting for me at the kitchen table. She shook her head at me, and I couldn't take anymore talking. I wanted quiet. I walked right up to her, kissed her on the cheek, and told her I was going to bed. I was starting to feel just how tired I really was.

By the time I washed my face and returned back to my bed, my mom had brought in a sandwich and a glass of milk and set it next to my bed. Thankfully, she wasn't still waiting in there for me. I scarfed down the sandwich and slugged back the milk. I took off my socks and wormed my way in between my sheets

I had no problem falling asleep.

## CHAPTER 8:

## BACK ON THE RIGHT TRACK

*Everything was dark. I felt like I had my arm stretched out right in front of me, but I couldn't see it. I turn my wrist back and forth, hoping to catch a glimpse of something. A tiny light snuck through a crack that I hadn't seen before. I reach my hand toward it, but have no strength, and slump back down.*

*I hear a faint tapping noise, somewhere close, but can't move my body. I hear a voice nearby, "I'm sorry. Eat some food." I'm so confused. My mind is racing, my heart is pounding, and my body seems paralyzed.*

*Then, I'm just a visitor in another world, not my world. I'm back watching the little boy. Who is he? He's not so little anymore. He seems about thirteen or so, much older than the last dream. Is this even the same boy? I study his face. His brown eyes seem deep, and his light brown hair is longer now that he's older. It's sloppy, but doesn't look bad. He has a few freckles on his nose, and a typical teenage boy farmer's tan. He looks sad now as he sits on the couch of what looks like his living room with his baseball uniform on. I hear him blurt out, "Dad, am I adopted?" I don't see anybody else in the room with him, but his father must be within earshot. There is a long silence, and then, "Reagan, why would you even ask that, son?" I can only see Reagan sitting on the couch because there is a wall blocking my view into the kitchen, where his father must be standing.*

*"I dunno. It's just some guys on the team were kinda teasing me about it, and I dunno." I heard the boy respond.*

*"That doesn't even make sense, son. What do you tell them? Tell them to mind their own business, and stay focused on the game. Maybe if they focused more you guys would have a better record," the man said.*

*"Yeah, I guess. So, I'm not adopted then?" the boy pushed on.*

*"Kiddo, no, cut it out. I don't want to hear about this again, OK?" the father said a little more sternly this time, with a hint of uneasiness.*

I woke up abruptly and glanced over at my clock. At least a few hours had passed although it seemed like only minutes. I wasn't tired, and I was up and ready to go, so I grabbed my cell to call Nate, but then figured since it was only 4 a.m., I'd better give him a few more hours before I called to tell him about my latest dream.

I needed to figure out what they meant. The first part, being in the dark, and being weak, had to be about Natalie. I felt so strongly that I was in her body somehow, that at least she was alive, extremely weak, but alive. I opened up my desk drawer and snatched out a notebook. I should probably write these dreams down. If they are clues, then I don't want to get them mixed up or forget anything, especially since I am still having those dreams about this boy, whose name I now know is Reagan. I jotted everything down quickly, and tried to remember everything that has happened so far, beginning with the dream the night Natalie went missing, all the way up to finding her bracelet in Deep Creek today.

I wonder what the cops did with the bracelet. I was so excited to find it, but it really doesn't offer any more clues about Natalie except that maybe she was in the woods and somehow her bracelet came off. I shut the notebook and looked out my window into my yard. It was still very dark, but I thought I saw a light coming from the bushes. I squinted and looked again. Yup, it definitely seemed like a flashlight. I darted downstairs and outside.

I wondered if this was another gut feeling. Was the light real? Or was my subconscious making this up? I didn't know. I really didn't know what was going on with myself. I'm not a psychic, my dreams don't give me insight into the future--- they never have--- I didn't think they did at least. As I was walking out into the yard, I stopped suddenly as something hit me. Not a physical object, but a memory, kind of. I remembered that a very long time ago, I had believed in my dreams and what they were telling me. I shook my head, hoping to remember more, but it faded.

I kept walking into the yard with no real aim, figuring the light must have been nothing when I heard a voice, "Kennedy?"

"Yes?" I responded.

Just then, Nate appeared out of the bushes with a flashlight. So it was real! "What are you doing here, Nate? Do you know what time it is?" I asked.

"Yeah, do you? Looks like you couldn't sleep either," he shot back.

"Actually, I did sleep. I completely passed out, and I had two more dreams, I was going to call you, but I figured you were asleep."

"Well, I couldn't. I think I slept for like 15 minutes. My mom reamed me out for an hour after you dropped me off," Nate said, looking defeated.

"Did you tell her what we found though?" I asked, hoping this would help.

"Yeah, I told her everything, my dad too. They didn't care; they didn't want to hear anything I had to say. They just yelled and yelled, and Kennedy?" he said sheepishly with his eyes glancing upward to look me straight in the face.

"Yeah?"

Nate dropped the bomb on me, "They told me I couldn't see you or talk to you anymore."

"What are you talking about? Why me? What? No, you're obviously not going to listen to them, are you?" I asked. I didn't want to lose Nate. I had no one in this with me. No one understood. Nate probably didn't even really understand, but he accepted me, and believed me. All the parents think I'm a quack and that I've lost it since my best has disappeared. Nate was the only one left I could trust and confide in.

"Kennedy, I'm sorry, but I have to listen to them. I'll try and text you, but they said they are going to check my phone, and take it away if need be. Maybe we got too far into this thing, maybe we should back off. Maybe you should back off. I don't want this to end up tearing us apart. I don't want to lose another friend. I can't. I'm done," he finished his rant.

I was completely devastated. I was mad at Nate. No, not really mad at Nate, none of this was his fault. His parents don't understand, but neither do mine. My mom thinks I need a shrink and meds, and his parents have always disliked me, and now that I'm dragging their son into this stuff, I really couldn't blame them.

Image is everything around here, and Nate's parents were well aware of that little game. I tried to quickly think up a plan, a way for me to stay in touch with Nate without getting him into more trouble. I thought texting would be safe, but they were going to check. My mind was jumbled, and I couldn't think straight. Nate must have known what I was doing and he said he had a plan. He told me that he would switch my name in his phone to another name, any name, just in case his parents checked. Just then, I realized I hadn't even told him about my dreams, and the name Reagan popped into my mind. I told him to enter me as Reagan in his phone, and he'd know it was me. If his parents asked, he was going to tell them it was a friend he met online going to the same college next year. He was a dork like that, so his parents would believe that story.

Once we had that figured out, I quickly recapped my two dreams, the one in the darkness, and then the boy Reagan that I always dreamt of. He didn't offer any real insight into my dreams, but he did say that he thought maybe they did mean something afterall. He believed my gut feeling this afternoon led us to the bracelet, and to have the same types of dreams so many times had to be for a reason. I was so happy and relieved that he seemed to believe the same things I did about my dreams and feelings.

The sun started to creep up in the distance and Nate had to get home before his parents woke up. I looked back in toward the kitchen and saw that my mom was already up and staring at us. I said goodbye to Nate, which was sadder than normal considering I wasn't sure if I'd be able to have regular contact with him now. He asked me to let him know if I had any more dreams or heard anything from the cops. I agreed, then walked back into my house.

"Good morning," my mom chirped.

"Morning, Mom. What are you doing up so early?" I asked.

"It's not that early, honey, it's 6 a.m., that's when I always get up," she responded.

"Oh, yeah, I guess that's right."

"I received a phone call from the police last night after you stomped up to your room."

"I didn't stomp, Mom, I was tired," I cut in.

"Not important," she said. "What is important is that the police have had just about enough of you and Nate getting too involved. They humored you yesterday when you were rude and condescending to them at the station, and then you both going back to Deep Creek hoping to find God knows what is just completely unacceptable," my mom said, sounding mad for the first time in a very long time. She went on. "I didn't say much last night when you got home, but you are like a different person, someone I don't even know any more, Kennedy. I know you have a lot going on, and are so worried about Natalie, but you have to trust that the police are doing everything they possibly can. And you running around interfering is just taking time and energy away from their investigation."

My mom had actually made a good point. I felt bad for the first time. I still think the police were not doing their jobs the best they could, even though I'm sure Natalie's parents were all over them, but I wasn't being any help by making them babysit me.

"I know, Mom. I am really upset over Natalie and just want to help if I can. I never meant to interfere, I want her found as badly as anyone," I sheepishly replied.

"I know, hon, I know. I'm just worried. Worried about Natalie, worried about you, especially about you."

"Why are you worried about me?" I asked.

"Kennedy, you have barely slept. I thought you slept last night, but clearly you didn't. You say you are having these dreams, I'm afraid that you're really heading down an unhealthy path."

"I did sleep last night!" I protested.

"OK, one night. Why don't you try those pills the doctor prescribed, let's try one today during the day, and a sleeping pill tonight. How about it?" my mom asked.

I hadn't picked up the pills yesterday, that was just my cover story for going to Deep Creek. My mom already knew this though, and she nodded her head toward the coffee maker, and there was a bag from our pharmacy with my name on it. She must have gotten them yesterday once she realized I was not where I said I was.

"Oh, um, can I just try on my own, see if I sleep tonight?" I asked.

"Honey, why don't you just try? It won't hurt you, come on," my mom prodded.

"Mom, seriously, come on, just let me see if I sleep tonight. I slept last night, I swear I did. I got up at 4, that's all," I replied.

"OK, OK, we'll talk about this later. Since we're both up, can I make you some breakfast?" my mom asked.

"Yeah, that sounds good, thanks Mom."

I must have been hungrier than I thought, because I ate three eggs, bacon, and toast. My mom also gave me a huge glass of orange juice, my favorite. I asked for a refill of OJ, and about halfway through my second glass, I got very tired. I was just sitting at the kitchen table, but I could feel my eyelids closing little by little. My mom must have seen this because she said I looked tired. I protested that I was fine, but she told me to go lay down on the couch in the living room. I barely remember getting to the couch and plopping down.

*Darkness again. I immediately looked for the small crack of light. It was still there. I reached out my hand toward it again, and this time I felt a little stronger. I ran my finger down the crack and at the bottom I felt something cool. I grabbed it. It was a plate with crumbs on it. I was becoming more aware of exploring the dream I was having, I could feel it. I scooted closer to the light, and tilted my head to peer through the opening. I saw more light, and grass. I scanned quickly to see if I could see anything else. I strained both my eyes so far they started to hurt. I thought I saw something small and round, and white, but I couldn't make out what it was. My shoulders dropped down, I was so tired. Why was I so tired from moving two inches? "Hello," I managed to make my lips push out a word. My voice sounded different though. It was dry, and crackly, and not mine. I spoke again, "Hello, is anybody there?" I asked. The voice was so familiar; it was Natalie's voice, coming out of my mouth. Or was it Natalie's mouth?*

*Back in that house again, it was becoming familiar to me. No one was in the kitchen this time. I had a bird's eye view of the kitchen, living room, hallway, staircase, and now a study. It was a typical office workspace. The desk had a large computer on it, a few picture frames, and paper sprawled out messily. I spotted Reagan sitting behind the computer in the chair. He was in his baseball uniform again. At first I could only see his face. He was squinting his eyes slightly, concentrating hard on what was on the computer screen. I so wished I could see what was on the screen. I wanted to know more about him, and why he had been in my dreams for so many years and why now, when I so desperately needed to help Natalie. As if by command, the view changed so that I was standing behind Reagan and I could see the computer screen perfectly. Reagan was on an adoption website. He was scanning the home page, and clicked on the contact page. He found an email address link, and clicked it, taking him to his mail. He stopped suddenly, minimizing the mail window, he turned to the office door, which was closed, and waited. A minute went by, and he twisted back and re-opened the mail window. He typed a short note, with a subject line of "past adoption records." The letter was as follows:*

*Hello, I am sorry to bother you, but I was wondering if your agency could provide me with some information. My wife and I adopted our son many years ago, and we were wondering if we could get some information on his biological parents. He wants to get in touch. Our son's name is Reagan, and he is fifteen years old. Thank you.*

*Sincerely,*
*Carl Edwards*

*Carl Edwards? That must be Reagan's dad. So, Reagan didn't believe his dad when he told him before that he wasn't adopted. I wonder why those kids were even asking if he was adopted? I never asked anyone that in my life. I looked at a picture that was on the desk to see if Reagan looked like his dad, but just as I saw the picture, Reagan jumped up, tripped a bit on the side of the desk, and ran out of the office. I followed. He got out of the office just as his father, Carl Edwards, was walking through the front door, which was only a few feet away.*

My eyes were trying to force themselves open, but they were sticky. "Mom?" I cried out. I was confused as to where I was. Was this a dream? "Mom?" I yelled out again.

"Yes, honey, I'm here, are you OK?" she asked. She was in the kitchen, but quickly came into the living room.

"Mom? Yeah, I'm OK, I'm just a little disoriented. Why am I so tired?" I asked.

"Oh, honey, you've had a few long days, and haven't slept much, it's just catching up with you. Do you want some water?" she asked, caringly.

"No. What time is it?" I asked, as I sat up, with my head spinning a little.

"Oh, it's 3 p.m., dear."

What? I was sleeping for like eight hours? I must have been really tired. I almost feel bad that I slept so long, I feel like I should be up trying to figure stuff out for Natalie. At least I had that dream again, but somehow I'm still just as confused. I stood up, knowing I needed to jot down my dreams before I forgot the details.

"Where are you going, Kennedy?" my mom asked.

"Oh, just upstairs, I need to grab something," I said. I ran upstairs and into my room. I jotted down the details of my last two dreams, trying to remember everything because I didn't know what might be important later. I just finished and shut my notebook when I heard a knock on the door. It was my mom. She seemed happy that I had slept, and was probably relieved. She told me she spoke with Nate's mom and his mom told her that she didn't think it was healthy for Nate and I to be talking as much as we did. They were both worried for their children's health. I didn't understand this at all.

I was getting to my mom-speak limit, and had to interrupt to get to the real news. I asked her if she had heard from the cops. She hadn't. I asked her if she would go down to the station with me so I could ask if they figured anything out from the bracelet yesterday. She did not want to. I begged and pleaded. I think she was afraid to leave me alone, so she finally agreed that she'd go with me. I'd like to think my mom knew me well enough that if I was passionate about something, I was going to do it. She probably figured it was safer to have me under her watchful eye.

The station seemed like it was much busier than yesterday. The receptionist rolled her eyes when we told her who we were, and who we wanted to see. Nonetheless, she led us to a desk. There was a police officer I had yet to meet, but he told us he could provide us with a few more details. He seemed a lot nicer than the previous officer, but I wasn't getting my hopes up. He told us about the bracelet, and how they had run it for any prints. He started speaking in CSI code and it was all very hard to follow, but I did get that the only prints they found on it were Natalie's, and a partial print that they figured to be mine. This made sense because she was always twirling it and playing with it on her wrist. He did say that because the bracelet was found in the woods, and under a rock, it did lead them in a new direction. They seemed sure that someone else had been involved that night, and that Natalie didn't leave on her own accord.

Duh! I knew they were not doing their jobs. I tried to tell them this so many times in Deep Creek and here. Natalie didn't just leave on her own. I told this officer that I didn't think she left on her own either. Someone had to have taken her, but I had no idea who. The officer just nodded politely in my direction and continued on. He said Kyle had been cleared, but they were still questioning everyone as to who else could possibly have interacted with Natalie that night.

I asked about the older man that no one knew. The police officer's eyes lit up.

"What older man?" he asked.

"I told the officer in Deep Creek that night. Some kid at the party said he saw Natalie outside talking to some older guy. Tanner," I told him.

"Tanner was the older man's name?" he asked.

"No, no, no. Tanner is a kid in our grade. He was outside Friday night and said he saw Natalie talking to some older guy. He figured he was someone's father picking them up, but he didn't recognize him."

Why weren't these cops even looking into this? I mean, it probably was someone's dad, but maybe he saw something that no one else did.

"I don't have this in my notes at all. Are you sure there was someone else there? This Tanner kid saw him? I don't even have a Tanner in my notes," the officer said, shuffling through his papers on his desk.

"Yeah, I'm sure. I mean, he probably was someone's dad, but can't you guys figure out whose dad it was, because maybe he saw Natalie when she was in the woods, or saw something happen to her, I don't know," I said back.

"OK, you're going to have to excuse me, I need to speak to someone. We'll be in touch later. We have your number. Thank you, Kennedy," he told me. He seemed sincere. His eyes were scanning back and forth over his papers, with his one hand already on his phone.

We excused ourselves and left the station. My mom, for the first time, looked at me like I was useful. Maybe I just helped this investigation. It seemed like some important things got lost in the shuffle between the Deep Creek and local police. I just hope that this mystery dad saw something useful that can help us find Natalie. Whenever I said her name, I could feel almost a tinge in my stomach. My shoulders felt like they had bricks weighing on them. My head felt light. I knew she was getting weaker. We had to find her soon. I didn't want to think about what would happen to my best friend if we didn't find her soon.

## CHAPTER 9: NIGHTWALKER

When we arrived home, I stayed by the phone. I knew I was being naïve, but I half expected the officer to call back quickly, I still held onto the hope that the police had a lead on the mystery dad, and that somehow he saw what happened to Natalie.

My mom was scurrying around the kitchen, cleaning up, wiping the tables down, filling up the dishwasher, obsessively placing each dish in its proper place, and making sure everything fit in exactly right. She did this when she was nervous, or bored. Right now she may have been both. I was spinning my cell phone on the counter top, hoping I'd hear back from Nate. I texted him on the way home from the police station, telling him what had just happened, but I hadn't heard back from him yet. I felt anxious and alone. I wasn't sure what my next step should be.

I decided that a walk would do me good. I told my mom, and she tried to persuade me to stay in and eat some dinner. I told her I'd eat when I got back, but she wouldn't take no for an answer. She definitely didn't want to let me out of her sight, so I agreed to eat a quick sandwich before my walk. I sat down to wait for my sandwich, but she suggested I go upstairs and wash up, and she'd bring the sandwich to me. I thought that was kind of weird, but I just did what she said because the faster I ate this sandwich, the faster I could go on my walk and think about what to do next.

I ran upstairs, washed my face, and grabbed my notebook as I sat on my bed. I looked over my last few notes, seeing if anything jumped out at me. I was hoping that some sort of sign would come out of the pages. If I did have some sort of psychic ability, now was the time to use it.

I started to wonder if these signs would only come to me in my dreams. I had accepted the fact that what I saw in my dreams was purposeful, at least with Natalie, but I still wasn't sure about the boy, Reagan. I had felt a pulling on my arm down in the woods at Deep Creek, but besides that, I hadn't really gotten any type of feeling when I was conscious. I don't know what I expected, but nothing was jumping out at me. I tossed the notebook aside just as my mom came in with a sandwich and a glass of soda. I don't know why she was catering to me so much. I realized a while ago that she no longer trusted me, although she obviously felt bad for what I was going through.

I was expecting her to drop off the food and leave, but she lingered in my room, hovering over me. I felt uncomfortable and told her so, and she said she would just feel better if she knew I had eaten. I thought she was being weird, but I took a few bites and a few swigs of soda.

She started up again about not interfering with the investigation, but I wanted none of it. I kind of blocked her out as I ate some more of my sandwich. I just kept nodding my head with an uninterested smile. It must have been working because she kept talking to me as if I was really listening. I could only think about finishing and going on my walk, getting out of this house. I finished the sandwich, but could tell my mom was still watching me closely, eerily. I looked over and saw that my soda was still nearly full. I grabbed it, obliging my mother, and took a few big gulps leaving nothing behind. I set it down hoping that would appease my mom.

I started to stand up and felt faint so I sat back down.

"Are you OK, honey?" my mom asked seemingly concerned.

"Yeah, I just feel a little funny," I could barely get up. I slouched back into my pillows on my bed. My mom lifted up my feet so I was completely lying on my bed.

"Why don't you take it easy for a few minutes, maybe you're still tired. Rest your eyes," my mom said as she stroked my hair. I barely heard her finish her sentence, and I was out.

*I was flying again, but this time it wasn't the wooded, expansive outdoors of Colorado, but a suburban area. I flew over houses that looked a lot like my neighborhood. I saw people grilling out back, kids playing tackle football, and cars gliding up and down the calm streets. Then I flew over some water, it looked like a river or lake, and it was narrow and long. Maybe it wasn't a river or lake, no, it looked more like a man-made pond. I then saw something weird. It was a square structure made of white columns with a black opening in the middle. It looked familiar, like something I'd seen in pictures before, if not in person, but I was too far away to tell. Then, everything went dark again. I braced myself for exploring in Natalie's body again, but I was light, I didn't have the feeling that I was in anyone's body, but that I was floating around completely unattached. I thought I heard something, and looked around. I couldn't see anything, but then I heard the voice. "You're doing so well, Kennedy. Keep going." It was definitely Natalie's voice. I looked around for her, but there was only* darkness. "Natalie, are you ok?" I asked, but got no response. I couldn't communicate with her, but maybe she was sending me messages. I tried again, "Nat, where are you?" hoping I'd get the jackpot with this one, but nothing. I heard her voice one more time, and it was a warning that shocked me, "Stop letting your mom make your food, she's drugging you," and that was it. I had been so stupid; of course she was slipping me Ambiens, that's why I was getting so devastatingly tired after each meal.

  With a snap of the fingers I was back to Reagan's house. Reagan was alone again in his dad's office at the computer. I was behind him again, anxiously trying to read his email as his clumsy fingers hurried to type in the email information. I glanced up at the picture frame on the desk, the one I had tried to look at last time, and it was still there. It was a picture of Reagan and his father, Carl Edwards, at a baseball game. They both had on red caps with a cursive "W" on it. I didn't know if this was significant, but I willed myself to remember it to put it in my notebook when I woke up. Carl was a pretty good looking man, for a dad, I guess. His light hair contrasted with his son's, and his pale skin looked more like Natalie's shading than Reagan's. But the pair looked happy. Reagan didn't look much younger than he did now, so the picture must have been fairly recent, I thought. I glanced back up to the computer and Reagan had an email up and was scanning it. The email read:

 Dear Mr. Edwards,
  Thank you for writing us to get in touch with a family, but I'm sorry to inform you that you must be mistaken. We have no record of a boy named Reagan who would be fifteen years old. Your name and information are not in our system. Could you be contacting the wrong adoption agency? This does happen from time to time. Please let us know if we can help you in any other way, and we wish you the best of luck in your search.

*Reagan looked confused, and angry. He deleted the email quickly, and then pulled out a piece of paper from his pocket. This was the first time I had seen Reagan at this age not wearing a baseball uniform. The piece of paper had a list of names, which seemed to be names of adoption agencies. There were five agency names, and four of them had a line through the name. Reagan drew a line through the fifth and final name. He looked defeated. Reagan quickly bounced up out of the chair, out of the office, slammed the door, and ran up the spiral stairs and into his room. The room was a typical teenage boy's room. There were posters of athletes and pretty models hung on the wall. His baseball gear was over in the corner, and his schoolbooks were sprawled out on the floor. He walked over to his bed and sat down. He grabbed the baseball sitting on his comforter and started to toss it up in the air and catch it. He repeated this action, gripping the ball tighter and tighter each time he caught it. Then, all of a sudden, he threw the ball with all his rage out his bedroom window. The ball went violently crashing through the window.*

I instinctively covered my face, as I could still hear the window breaking, and almost feel the glass shattering all over me. My room was dark. Why was my mom drugging me? Where was she? What time was it? Where was my notebook? So many questions were running through my head. I hopped up and flipped on my bedroom light. I surveyed the room looking for my notebook to write down the dreams I just had before I forgot them.

I wrote down everything I could remember furiously, as if I was forgetting it as quickly as I was writing it down. My notes seemed almost unreadable, and I hoped I'd be able to make them out later, if I needed to. I went to reach for my cell phone, but it wasn't on my nightstand next to my bed. I glanced around the room, and saw that my mom had plugged it into the charger over on my desk. I didn't like her touching my stuff, but I was thankful that I now had a full charge on my cell. The time shocked me; it was 3 a.m., Tuesday morning now. It took me a minute to remember which day it was. The past three days have felt like a lifetime to me. My life had changed so much in that time period; it almost felt like a dream. I froze for a second. Was this a dream? Was I somehow having a dream within a dream like in that movie *Inception*? I had no Leonardo DiCaprio to guide me through this. I picked up my phone to call Nate, because I didn't care what time it was, I had to know if I was still dreaming, and if I wasn't then I needed to tell him about my last dream.

The phone rang twice, and then it sounded like someone answered, and immediately hung up. Nate could have been sleeping and inadvertently hung up on me, or his parents had confiscated his phone. I waited a minute, then texted him. I realized he hadn't texted me back from earlier on in the day. This wasn't a good sign. I quickly typed in "SOS are you there?"

A minute waiting seemed like forever, but I got a response, "Yes, are you okay?"

I typed back, "YES! More dreams, I'm coming over." I didn't even wait for a response. I grabbed my notebook, flung it and my cell phone into my backpack and walked out of my room. I somehow had forgotten that my mom had drugged me until that very instant, and I ran back into my room to look at the soda glass. It was still on my desk with the empty plate. At the bottom of the glass, I could see a little white powder clinging to the glass and the tiniest bit of soda left. There was my proof! How could she do this to me? It was unforgivable, but I didn't have time to confront her now, I just knew I wouldn't be drinking anything else that woman gave me!

I had planned on walking over to Nate's on the streets, since we lived so close, but something told me to go the back way. It wasn't a voice, a vision, or a pulling like in Deep Creek, just a feeling. I decided to listen, and walk around the side of my house to the back yard. I was walking through my yard and I noticed a baseball. How did this get here? Strange. I obviously didn't play baseball, and my neighbors on each side were both a lot older, I'm talking like mid eighties and older, I didn't think they'd be tossing the ball around any time soon. We've never found a stray object from our neighbor's in our yard, ever. I noted the weirdness, and was going to just walk by, but I couldn't leave it. My leg swung back and my foot connected with the ball, kicking it slightly in front of me. As soon as my shoe touched the ball, my body jolted. It felt like a lightning bolt had hit me. I got a quick flash of the window breaking in Reagan's room- then a quick flash of Natalie's bracelet in the woods, glittering when the sun hit it- back to a flash of the baseball now sitting in a sun-filled yard, not my own- then another flash of Natalie's face.

    I felt different. I checked my arms and felt my face, making sure that something had not actually struck me. It was still the dark of night, and I was still in the yard. The baseball was now a few feet in front of me. I wanted to pick it up, or kick it again, but was honestly afraid of the getting that jolt again. I stared at the baseball for another minute or so, then felt my phone vibrate. It was a text from Nate, asking where I was, I should have been at his house by now. With that, I shoved my phone back into my backpack, ignored the ball, and cut through the remaining yards, getting to Nate's house as fast as possible.

    When I arrived, I found Nate sitting on a chair on his back patio. He seemed tired, and a little angry that I woke him up at this hour, but I didn't care, I had to tell him everything that had just happened. I excitedly told him about the dreams I had been having, how Natalie spoke to me, and was weak somehow, and about Reagan, and the baseball flash I had just had, and Nate kept reminding me to keep my voice down. His parents might kill me if I woke them up and they knew I was here talking to Nate.

Nate listened to every word I said, and got very interested when I told him about the baseball. He tried to reason why the ball would be in my yard in the first place, and we honestly couldn't figure out one realistic soluttion. He then got excited and asked me, "Kennedy, do you think you could *make* yourself get some sort of vision, or flash, like you did with the baseball? And not just wait for a dream?"

I actually hadn't even thought of it. The baseball flash was exhilarating, but scary, to be honest. I told him, "I'm not sure, Nate. I never thought of it. Do you think it could help?"

"Hell yes. Your dreams seem to be getting more vivid, giving you more clues, now imagine if you could make these visions come to you in other ways, when you're not sleeping. I think it could help a lot."

Now, I was the one reminding him to keep his voice down.

"I mean, maybe. It was kind of scary though, when I kicked the ball. It jolted me. I felt it, and the visions were much quicker, and it was hard to make them out. I got a little nauseous," I replied. I was almost talking myself out of it. I was afraid for some reason.

"I know, Kennedy, I don't mean to push, but I think we've gotta explore this. Did you bring the ball?" he asked.

"Shoot, no. I thought about it, but was a little scared to touch it again. We can go back to my house, and you can watch me touch it again," I suggested.

"Yeah, let's do that. We have a lot to do in a few hours before everyone else gets up and I'm on lock down again," he said and jumped out of the chair.

We started running through his yard, and back toward my house, and in two minutes we were back to my yard. The baseball was nowhere in sight.

"It was right here, I swear," I pointed to the spot and told him.

"Well, where is it now? Where could it be?" he asked, confused.

"I don't know. Look, I kicked it a few feet, and it was right here when I came to your house."

"I believe you, chill, all I'm saying is where could it possibly be now? I'll look over here, you look on the other side," Nate suggested.

We both looked for a solid five minutes, and even searched the front of the house, but no luck, the ball was gone. This just added to the mysteriousness of the entire incident.

"Maybe you should mark that down in your journal," Nate suggested.

"Shut up," I replied. I thought he was being sarcastic, but he wasn't.

"No, I'm serious. You said that in your dream that Reagan boy threw a ball through his window, right? And then when you kicked it, part of your flash was the ball breaking the window? It could be related, right?" Nate asked eagerly.

"Actually, maybe."

"Do you think it works kind of like he threw it, and it landed in *your* yard?" Nate asked again.

I was stumped. I didn't know how this all worked. First it was the dreams that didn't make sense, then the pulling, now a time warped baseball? It was almost too much. I plopped down in the grass. Nate came over beside me and put his hand on my shoulder.

"Listen, I know this is a lot for you, and you're the one who's experiencing it all. Natalie's gone, your mom is drugging you, and I haven't been the most supportive friend. It's gotta be hard on you, I get it. But, Kennedy, I really think you're on to something. Your dreams, your gut feelings, and now these flashes of visions, it's got to mean something. It's all got to be related, even this boy you've been dreaming about. We don't know how yet, but it's got to be clues somehow, and I think you're the only one who may be able to get Natalie back, so you can't stop now, OK?" Nate said, looking down into my eyes, his own filling with soft tears.

I had never seen Nate cry before, and I'm not sure you could even classify this as crying, but his eyes looked gentle and comforting in the summer moonlight. I believed him, and it made me believe in myself more. I was done going to the cops, and they weren't going to find me interfering anymore. I may interfere, but I was done being sloppy and letting them catch me. I would figure this out, find Natalie, and bring her home. Nate will help me, and we will take this into our own hands. I was confident in my abilities now, whatever they may be, but I had to come up with a plan, and quick, because we only had another hour or so before the sun came up, and then we had to deal with our parents.

## CHAPTER 10:

## HISTORY REPEATS ITSELF

By the time the sun came up, Nate and I were back in our respective houses. I was sitting at the kitchen table when my mom came down for her morning coffee.

"Hello, Nadene," I tersely whispered. She jumped, apparently startled that I was down here before her.

"Good morning, Kennedy, how did you sleep, honey?" she responded back.

"Oh, excellent. It felt like I was drugged or something," I chatted back, emphasizing the word "drugged."

"Oh, don't be so dramatic, but I'm glad you slept well. Can I make you breakfast to start your day?"

"No thanks. I started my day hours ago actually, and I'm not too into the idea of letting you prepare my food or drinks for the near future, you know, considering you did in fact drug me, twice," I spat back.

My mother looked shocked, for which I have no explanation since she was the one who drugged me twice in 24 hours, and then thought I would never figure it out.

"How did you?" I cut her off.

"How did I know? Well, there was some powder still left in my soda glass from last night that you forgot to clean up, and the fact that I never sleep that much, especially in the past few days, oh, and" I started to tell her that I heard in my dream, but I stopped myself. I wasn't sure I wanted to let my mom in on the fact that I believed my dreams were giving me hints about Natalie's disappearance.

"And what?" she asked me.

"Nevermind," I shrugged, as I opened the refrigerator, grabbed a Gatorade and headed toward the front door.

"Where are you going, Kennedy?" my mother asked, clinging on to any authority she may still have left.

"Out." I walked through the front door, ready to try out my theories on this potentially psychic ability I may have stumbled upon. My mother didn't follow me, nor did she call my phone. I can only imagine what she was doing after I left, but I think I made it clear I was no longer listening to her guidance. She betrayed me, and I'd had enough.

Nate and I had thought up different scenarios of what we, mostly I, could do to try to bring these visions on. The obvious idea was going back to Deep Creek, walking around, touching something that Natalie may have touched, but that wasn't really possible. We figured that if the ball mysteriously appeared in my yard again, I'd definitely try to touch it, but as of this morning, the ball was nowhere in sight.

We also thought that maybe I could try to talk to Kyle again. He was one of the last people in contact with Natalie, and maybe that would trigger a flash of some sort. This was still possible, but Kyle was not too thrilled to have ever known me at this point. The cops had given him a pretty rough time questioning him. Still, this was an option. Another option was going over to Natalie's house, asking the Hall's if I could go into her room for a minute or two, but this required me attempting to explain why I wanted to sit in her room, or touch her things.

The Hall's had always liked me, and although our families were definitely classes apart, Mrs. Hall always treated me very well, like a second daughter. I think she figured I was helping set a good example for Natalie. I was still worried about trying to explain myself to them, so I rode my bicycle to Kyle's house first. I knocked on the door and Kyle's father answered.

"Who are you?" he asked, roughly.

"Hi, I'm Kennedy, I'm a friend of Kyle's," I half lied.

"Well, what do you want?" he asked back.

"Um, sorry, can I speak to him just for a quick second, please?" I asked in the most polite way I could muster.

Kyle opened the door and scooted his dad aside. He scrunched up his nose as he glared at me. "What do you want?" he asked.

"Kyle, sorry to bug you, but can we talk a minute?" I asked.

"No, get lost, you already tried to ruin my life," he yelled. He started to shut the door, but I quickly shoved my hand out to stop the door from shutting in my face.

"Kyle! Please! I need your help!" I begged.

He opened the door a slight bit, just enough to say, "My help? Screw you, Kennedy! You've always hated me, always, and now you're blaming me for all this. Screw you!" he yelled, and slammed the door with vengeance.

As the door slammed, a rush of wind flew my way and I froze. Another flash, but no lightning bolt jolt this time, thankfully. Kyle slamming the door in Natalie's face- *flash*- Natalie crying on the doorstep- *flash*- Reagan crying in his room, staring at his broken window- *flash*- Natalie crying in a small, dark, wooden room- *flash*- Reagan sitting in his bed, hands and feet duct taped- *flash-flash-flash-flash-flash-flash*.

I was on the ground with my hands over my ears, trying to stop the bangs from penetrating my eardrums as each flash of bright light hit me.

The door opened, "You're a freak, get the hell out of here," Kyle yelled, and slammed the door again.

That was too much for me. I was in way over my head. I ran over to my bike and pedaled away as fast as I could. I pedaled in no direction specifically, and after a few minutes, I slowed to a stop. I sat on the closest sidewalk, and broke out my notebook. I recounted my last flash experience, and how I felt. My reactions were becoming more intense to the visions and flashes I was having. Could these hurt me physically? I really didn't know, but I was starting to become concerned.

I did figure out that certain situations that related to Natalie triggered these flashes. She must have stood outside Kyle's door countless times, having the door slammed in her face by her boyfriend, crying helplessly. When he slammed the door in my face, that must have been the trigger. I really had to explore how Reagan fit into this whole situation though. When I saw Natalie crying, I then saw Reagan crying. This poor kid is obviously upset about something, and is convinced that his dad, Carl Edwards, isn't his biological father. I felt bad for him, I really did, I just didn't understand why he was taking up half of my dream and vision time when I needed more clues about Natalie. I then remembered the last flash I saw of Reagan bound and seemingly being held hostage. However Reagan fit into this whole thing, I wasn't sure, but it seemed like this was happening somewhat in real time. Was he kidnapped too?

I thought for a second, and the best explanation I could think of was that this poor boy was kidnapped, and maybe his signals were getting mixed up with Natalie's. I wished his signals could go to the proper person, other people like me who could help him. I decided that I'd still keep track of Reagan's clues, or whatever you wanted to call them, and as soon as we found Natalie, I'd try my best to help him, and hope it wasn't too late.

A car whizzed by me while I was still on the sidewalk, and it shook me back into present time. Now that I knew that I had to find triggers to get more clues, I was convinced I had to go to Natalie's house. I rode the few blocks to the Hall's house, took a deep breath, and approached their front door.

Just as I was about to knock on the door, Mrs. Hall opened it up.

"Oh, Kennedy, hello," she greeted me.

"Mrs. Hall, hi, sorry to bother you, but could I come in for a minute?" I asked.

"Oh, I'm sorry, I was just leaving, can you come back in a few hours?" she replied.

"No, well, sorry, actually, is Mr. Hall home then?" I asked, hoping that someone was home so I could go explore Natalie's room for a minute.

"No, honey, he's not here. What's this all about, are you OK?" she asked, as she stepped out through the door.

"No, well, yes, I'm OK, I just, I'm so sorry about Natalie. Can I just run up to her room for a quick second?" I asked, leaving out the details about finding triggers.

"Oh, dear, yes, you probably have been wanting that sweatshirt you left from last week, don't you?" Mrs. Hall asked me.

I had completely forgotten about the Colorado hoodie I had left in Natalie's room from last week. It was the absolute last thing on my mind, but this was a perfect excuse for me to snoop around the room, unsupervised. I decided to run with it.

"Yes. I'm so sorry, I'll only be a second," I told her.

"No problem, dear, you know where it is. I have to run down to the police station, they said it's urgent, excuse me for leaving so abruptly," she quickly added.

Mrs. Hall was nothing if not exceedingly polite. "News? Have they found Natalie?" I asked, knowing this couldn't possibly be the case.

"No, dear," she started, sounding increasingly sad, and I was immediately sorry I suggested this was the reason they were calling her in. "I think they just want to ask me more questions. That's all they seem to be doing. But I did hear you snuck back down to Deep Creek and found her bracelet," she started.

"Yes, I'm sorry I interfered, I never wanted to hurt the investigation, I just wanted to help," I replied. I hoped she would understand.

"I know, honey. You were like a sister to Natalie, and I appreciate you trying to help, but I heard it was a dead end, no clues. But Kennedy, thank you for being such a good friend, dear," and with this, she ushered me in the house, and shut the door behind me.

I was relieved that she wasn't mad at me for trying to help, but I was unnerved at the tone of our conversation. It sounded like Mrs. Hall was giving up. It had only been a few days, and it sounded like she had no hope at all. This couldn't be true. Natalie was still alive. She may be weak, but she was alive. Every bone in my body told me so.

It felt weird being in Natalie's house without her. I had never done this before. I quickly walked up the stairs and into Natalie's room. Her house was set up a lot like mine, and I had been here close to a million times before, so it felt natural to stride into her room. But this time, she wasn't in it waiting for me. The Colorado sweatshirt was neatly folded on top of her wardrobe, but I could care less about that. I looked around the room, trying to see if I could find an obvious trigger. Nothing popped out at me, so I decided to touch a few different things and see if I got a flash like before.

I touched her notebook that was sitting out on her desk. I felt a shock like you get when someone rubs their feet on a carpet then touches you, a little static electricity. My eyes jammed shut and I saw Natalie sitting in calculus class, writing a note to Kyle. I lifted my hand, and then touched the notebook again, I got another flash of Natalie receiving her test back from Dr. Saunders; she got an A.

I slid my hand over to her snow globe that was at the corner of her desk. My eyes slammed shut again, and again I saw Natalie, but she was a little girl at Disney World with her parents, she was so happy. Whatever I was doing was working, I was getting flashes of Natalie, but not the right ones. I directed my touching to her closet. I slid my hands along her jeans and blouses hanging in the closet. Even though my hand only touched the clothes for a second each, I got many flashes. I saw Natalie riding a horse at her grandparent's farm, then I saw her sitting in the stands at one of Kyle's lacrosse games, then she was falling asleep in English class, and then eating dinner with her parents at a restaurant. The last piece of clothing I touched brought on a stronger feeling and flash. It was a summer dress that I recognized. Natalie had bought this dress only a few weeks ago, and was super excited about it. She told me all about it, and wore it to school the next day. The flash that accompanied the dress was of Natalie walking away from Kyle with tears in her eyes, then turning to be comforted by Nate. This flash was longer, and I saw more. Nate wiped away Natalie's tears gently from her cheeks, put his arm around her, and told her she looked too beautiful to cry, and they walked away with Natalie's head nuzzled into Nate's chest.

That flash made me smile, Nate was such a good friend to us, but I always thought he and I were much closer than he and Natalie, but I was glad to know he was so kind to her, especially when she was so sad.

Even with all those flashes, I still hadn't garnered any real clues. I decided to try and touch everything and see what I would get. I touched her shoes and got similar flashes to the clothes. I touched an umbrella and got a flashback of her walking through the rain to get to school, and then one of her using it as a sword in a pretend sword fight with her little cousin.

I touched a picture on the wall of Natalie and her parents holding her acceptance letter to Penn State. They were so proud she was going to their alma mater. I got a flash of the bracelet when her parents gave it to her, then a flash of the bracelet lying in the mud at Deep Creek, and then the bracelet sitting in a plastic bag in a storage container, I'm guessing at the police evidence room. I touched the next photo hanging up, a picture of me and Natalie when she got her hair cut a few months ago. She had donated her hair for Locks-of-Love, so they had to cut ten inches off in order to donate it for a wig for people with cancer. I thought it was so kind of her to do this, especially because Natalie was so attached to her hair. I joked with her that she was too vain to ever chop off her hair, and she was vain, but she also had a generous heart. Plus, she could make anything look good, so the ten inches off her blonde hair only made her seem more mature and trendy. We had the hairdresser snap a picture of me standing next to Natalie holding her ten inches of her ponytail she just got cut off. It was a really cute picture.

My eyes shut, and then I saw Natalie face down in what seemed to be a car, her hair matted to the side of her face as she was sweating, then a flash of Natalie crouched in a small room twirling her hair like she does when she's nervous. Her hair was longer than in the picture I was touching, so the image of Natalie was obviously recent, probably current, wherever she was now. This is the type of trigger I needed. I touched the rest of the photos, and everything else I could in her room, and although I was privy to visions of Natalie's past, nothing seemed to give me any clues as to where she was now.

In a last ditch effort, I touched the Locks-of-Love photo again, hoping to get another new flash, and I did. I saw Reagan, flipping his hair out of his eye as he sat on his bed, still tied up. This flash lasted a bit longer and stayed on Reagan. He kept swooping his head to his side to keep his hair out of his face, and he focused on the shed in his back yard. He stared at it until his eyes shut in desperate need of a blink, and just like that my flash was over. I touched the photo over and over again, but received no more flashes.

I had touched everything I could get my hands on in Natalie's room, and had no more luck with flashes. I definitely didn't want to be there when anyone came home, so I quickly wrote down what I had seen in my notebook, and left the Hall's house.

It was still early morning, and I had accomplished a lot, but I had no idea where Natalie was, besides that she seemed to be in a small area, and someone was holding her there against her will. I had a strange feeling about the last flash I had seen with Reagan peering out his window at a shed. Why was he so fixated on that shed? I still didn't know why Reagan was tied up either, I hope he is okay, but it was really starting to distract me from Natalie.

I texted Nate, updating him on my last two stops, but I didn't hear back from him. I hoped he fell asleep, he needed it. I'm sure I would need him later on in the day, but for now, I didn't know what was next, so I hopped on my bike and headed back home.

My mom was in the kitchen on the phone when I came in, so I quickly snuck up to my room, hoping she hadn't seen or heard me. I plopped down on my bed and reviewed my notebook from the beginning. There had to be something that would lead me in the right direction as to what to do next. These dreams and flashes were getting descriptive, but I wasn't any closer to figuring out where Natalie was.

I re-read my journal entry about Saturday morning in Deep Creek, and kept coming back to one thing: the older man who was someone's dad, or so we thought. I ripped out a clean sheet of paper and tried to write down every person that I remember being at the party that night. I didn't need to worry about people I saw in the morning, because if the man had been someone's dad, they would have already been taken home by him. I had a list of about fifteen people I could remember, not including myself, Nate, Natalie, Kyle, or Dax, the kid whose cabin it was. I probably had missed some people and thought about asking Kyle for help, but the last time I tried to talk to him he slammed the door in my face. I didn't know much about any of the other people on the list, and I certainly didn't know what their fathers looked like. I also didn't include Tanner because he was the one who said he saw the man. I put off calling Kyle at first, and pulled out the school directory. I called every person I remembered being at the party that night, and surprisingly, I got a hold of someone at each house. The problem was that everyone said it wasn't their dad, and they hadn't seen any man that night talking to Natalie. Then I got the same responses of why I was making these calls when the police should be doing it. My thoughts exactly.

When I had gone through my whole list, I had nothing left to do but call Kyle. I went to his number and pressed send. Surprisingly, he answered.

"What do you want now, Kennedy?" he asked, sounding pissed off still.

"Kyle, listen, I'm really sorry. I don't hate you, and I know you didn't do anything to Natalie, I really do. I just really want to find her and I need your help with something," I blurted out, not knowing how much time he would listen before he hung up. There was silence, but he was still on the line. "OK, I just made a list of people who were at the party. Remember how Tanner said he saw some older guy talking to Natalie that night? We figured it was someone's dad, so I want to call everyone and see if it was their dad."

"So you think this guy had something to do with taking Natalie?" he asked, sounding interested now.

"Maybe. Maybe not. But maybe if we can find him we will know what happened to Natalie or at least it will give us another lead," I quickly said.

"Why aren't the cops doing this?" he asked. Good question.

"I don't know. Tanner told the Deep Creek police, remember? But when I talked to an officer here, he hadn't heard of any of this, and didn't even have it in his notes, so I don't know. But, listen, I'll read you the names, and you tell me who else was there, OK? Please."

"OK. Go." He complied. I read him the list of names I had, and he was able to come up with about seven more people that I hadn't thought of, and to be honest, don't think I would even recognize if I saw them at the mall. I started looking up their phone numbers in the directory while I was still on the phone with Kyle.

"Thanks so much, Kyle. I'm going to call them all now and see what they know. Thanks again. I know we don't have the best relationship, but," he cut me off.

"But we both love Natalie," he said.

"Right," I said back. With that, we hung up, and I began to dial the next seven numbers on the list.

I had just finished calling the final number when my mom walked in.

"Hi," she simply said.

"Hi," I dryly responded back. I had nothing to say to her.

"Honey, listen, I'm sorry, I really am," she started to apologize.

"Mom, cut the shit, really. You drugged me, do you even get how terrible that is? I'm pretty sure I could call the cops on you, you know that, right?" I started in.

"Yes, I do. I am so sorry, but I only did it because I was so worried about you. There are things you don't remember, that you don't understand, and I want to protect you at all costs. I'm your mother for crying out loud," she barely got out as she started to cry. How did I end up comforting my mom after she betrayed and drugged me?

"Mom, don't cry. Listen, I'm eighteen, I've been through a lot. I think I'm handling myself well. You don't need to protect me at all costs that just sounds weird and dramatic.

I'm in no danger; Natalie is the one we need to worry about."

"I do, Kennedy. I worry about her all the time, but you are my daughter, and I need to worry about you too. You weren't sleeping, you were obsessing over things, and you were interjecting yourself into the investigation where you didn't need to be. These are not good signs," she said.

"Not good signs? Signs of what, Mom? I'm not having a mental breakdown if that's what you're worried about. My dreams have been helping me figure this all out. I didn't tell you this before, but I think I may be kind of psychic. I don't have it all figured out, but I get these gut feelings, like when I found the bracelet, and now sometimes when I touch things I get these type of flashes of past memories, and I've seen Natalie. She's definitely alive, but she's hurt and weak," I rambled on.

She just stood there, and her tears stopped, and whatever color she had left in her face had drained. "Dreams? Like you think you know where Natalie is? Or you spoke to her?" she asked me hesitantly.

"Yeah, well, kind of. It doesn't work that great, and I only get glimpses of things, and I don't know where she is, but I'm sure something is telling me to keep trying to find her, I just know it." I barely got this out of my mouth and my mom turned and left my room. I crept behind her to see what she was doing. Now I was worried about her. Her face was still ghostly white.

She grabbed the house phone in her room and dialed quickly. I heard her start a conversation without even saying hello, all she said was, "Jack, you need to get up here now. She is having dreams and visions and flashes, she just told me, you need to come immediately. She's remembering," and then she hung up the phone that quickly.

"Remembering what?" I asked, startling my mom. She obviously didn't know I was listening in on her conversation with my dad.

She jumped, and said, "Kennedy, you need to sit down. I need to tell you something. You need to stay calm. This is very important."

We walked back to my room and I sat on my bed. "Remember what?" I asked again, my voice rising as I was becoming more mad by the second. What was going on? My mom sat next to me and put her hand on my shoulder, and as soon as she touched me, I felt another jolt and my eyes slammed shut.

I was in a bedroom and I was myself, but as I looked at my own hands, they were small. I must have been a child, a small child. My cheeks felt wet, and my mom sat next to me, looking younger than she does now. She wiped away the tears from my cheeks, and rubbed my back. I felt like I was hyperventilating. Then I was in a candy store. I was standing on top of one of the lower containers of candy trying to reach the gummy worms, my childhood favorite. Then I was back in my bed, with my mom next to me, pleading with me to calm down, assuring me that I would be OK. Why was I crying? I couldn't stop. My body was shaking. "Where's brother Reagan?" I asked my mom. Back in the candy store, I hear a yell. I look back to see who yelled and my foot slips off the plastic container. I fall and slam my wrist on the metal opener where the candy comes out. My dad is screaming, turning his head around and around, he's yelling for the police, asking someone to get the police. I'm back in my room. Why was I asking for a brother? I don't have a brother. Reagan? Is this the boy I have been dreaming about my whole life? My mom keeps soothing my back, and I'm starting to breathe normally. She speaks softly, "He's gone, baby, he's gone."

## CHAPTER 11: THE PLAN

My eyes forced their way open, only to see my mom staring at me with her mouth wide open. I didn't let her get a word in before I started bombarding her with questions. "Did I? Do I have a brother? Did you guys hide this from me? What happened at the candy store when I was little? Who is Reagan? What is going on?" I spilled out.

My mom rose off the bed and was standing over me now with her hand over her mouth. I thought she might run away, so I jumped up and grabbed her shoulders and shook, "Mom, who is Reagan? Explain!" I screamed at her.

She started to cry again, still holding her one hand over her mouth. "I need to call your father back," she said, as she turned to leave. I tightened my hold on her shoulders and spun her back around to face me.

"No, Mom, you owe me this. Who is Reagan?" I figured we'd start with that. At this, my mom dropped her hand from her mouth and stood tall. She took a deep breath, and then began.

"Reagan is...was your brother."

"What? No, I don't have a brother, I've never had a brother," I protested, although all the signs were telling me I always had a brother, and I even remember the day he went missing. But how did I block this out for all of these years?

"No, honey, you *did* have a brother, his name was Reagan. He was kidnapped when you were three, and it was very hard on all of us." She started to get into the story, and I just let her talk. "That's why your father and I split up. Well, we had problems before, but that was the endpoint. The three of you were at the mall; Reagan was only a little over a year old then. I was getting my hair cut and your father took you two for a few hours. You were at the candy store, do you remember that store? Oh, you loved it. The bright colors, the smells, you just always had to go in there. Kennedy, you were climbing on some candy machines and your father turned to get you down, and he turned back to bring the stroller with Reagan in it with him, but the stroller was empty. It was horrible, honey. He only looked away for a second. Somebody screamed and said they saw a man take the baby out of the stroller. That's all your father remembers. We called the police immediately, of course, and we searched every inch of Philadelphia."

"Philadelphia?" I asked. I lived in the suburbs of Pittsburgh, not Philadelphia. We have lived in this house my entire life. My mom must have mistaken her P towns in Pennsylvania.

"Yes, Philadelphia, honey. We lived in Philadelphia before we moved here. Don't you remember? I guess you don't, that was the plan, it's what we had hoped for," my mother said.

"What plan? What are you talking about? I thought that we have always lived in this house, and then Dad moved out when you guys got a divorce, right?" I asked back.

"No. No, honey. We lived in Philadelphia, the four of us, and then Reagan was taken. We did everything we could. The news had his picture on TV all of the time. We had posters in every store, we searched every building, every park, every piece of the earth that we could possibly search. We had search parties working day and night. We were exhausted, and fighting, and were no closer to finding poor Reagan than the day he was taken. There were no security cameras in the mall, and no one got a good enough look at the man who took him. All we knew was that it was a man, in his early thirties, with kind of dirty blonde hair. That was it. It was horrible. Your father and I fought day and night, you, honey, were a mess. You missed your brother, and you didn't understand where he was, and you stopped sleeping. This is why I was so scared this time with Natalie when you weren't sleeping." I let my mother continue on. She had never talked this much in her life, and I didn't want to interrupt her train of thought, I needed to know it all. I was so confused.

"You used to fall asleep for an hour, and then wake up screaming in the middle of the night, saying you saw Reagan in your dreams. You said he was with a man, and he was OK, and happy, and that we shouldn't worry because the man loved him. Your father and I never slept, and we couldn't understand why you were telling us that this man loved our little boy. We tried to hold on to the idea that he was alive, and wasn't hurt, but we weren't given many positive signs from anyone, except you, saying that you had seen him and he was OK. You still missed him dearly, and then one night you woke up, crying hysterically, saying that you were sorry. You said in your dream that someone told you it was your fault, because you were climbing in the candy store and your father went to help you and left Reagan alone. You just cried and cried, and it wasn't your fault, Kennedy, it wasn't, but you were inconsolable. You weren't sleeping, you weren't eating, and you had this tremendous guilt that we couldn't understand a 3-year-old having. The only good decision your father and I made at that point was taking you to a child psychiatrist. The psychiatrist talked to you and told us that you were very intelligent and mature for your age, and that 3-year-olds didn't normally harbor guilt like you did. Your dreams were very vivid and you had a great imagination, but he was worried for your mental and physical development that you weren't going to progress because of your fixation on these dreams and guilt. He suggested an experimental procedure where we took you to get hypnotized, hoping we could rid you of the guilt. The hypnotist had never really worked on a child your age, but it was supposed to be good for relieving past feelings of guilt, and stopping negative dreams."

The more my mom talked, the more my old dreams started popping into my head. I had always had dreams about Reagan, but they were normal, and happy. He played in the same park, in the same sandbox, with the same smile on his face. Sometimes I would just see him smiling, or sleeping, but he was always fine, and seemed like a happy baby, then a young child. When I was in middle school, the dreams stopped for a while, but I really thought nothing of them. I hadn't dreamt of Reagan again until the night Natalie disappeared, and since then I've seen him grow into a young teenager, and not just as a small child. I let my mom go on.

"After that day with the hypnotist, we thought it helped you. You started to sleep longer each night, which let us sleep. Six months had gone by and we still had no lead on Reagan. Your father urged me to try and move on, but I couldn't. Every day, every second, was consumed by thinking of Reagan, and if we weren't searching for him I felt tremendous guilt. I stopped caring for you, for your father, for myself. He couldn't take it any longer and moved out. After a month, he filed for divorce. He decided to move to D.C., and it hurt him to be away from you, but being in Philadelphia just reminded him of his son who he would never see again. Every now and then you would tell me you saw Reagan in your dreams, but you didn't have that same guilt. After about a year, I realized I needed to move on and that you needed me. That's when we moved to Pittsburgh, to this home. The psychiatrist thought that if we moved, it might help you as well, and it really did. You didn't speak of Reagan, or of having any dreams of him after we moved here. I thought it was best for all of us if we never talked about him. It was so hard because you were my link to him, but I tucked it deep down inside me. No one here knew me, or us, or Reagan, so no one knew to ask. It was peaceful, and I thought our life would be better, and it has been, honey. I wanted to tell you so many times, but I never wanted to see you in pain like you were as such a young child. That's why I would do anything to protect you, and once I saw you starting to display the same signs, I took you to the psychiatrist and drugged you, which is inexcusable, I know." My mom finally stopped to take a breath.

It was so hard to take in everything I had just heard. My entire life, well I guess since I was three, I believed I was an only child, and that I was born and raised here in Pittsburgh. Now I find out that I have a brother, and we are from Philadelphia. I had a brother. Do I still have a brother? Is he still alive? I had to ask, although if I really believed any of my dreams or visions were true, I had to believe Reagan was still alive.

"Mom, is Reagan still alive?" I asked.

"Honey, we don't know. I'd like to think that he is, and I hope whoever took him treats him well, and that he doesn't realize he was ever kidnapped. It was so traumatic for everyone. But we don't know, and sometimes I fear the worst," she said.

"I think he is alive. I told you I had been dreaming. I've dreamt of Reagan a lot actually," I told her.

"What?"

"I have always dreamt of him. I didn't know it was him, of course. Even after I went to the hypnotist or psychiatrist or whatever, I always saw a little boy at a park," I started to tell her.

"I know, honey, that's what you always said when you were younger, after it happened," she interrupted.

"Yeah, yeah, but the dreams started up again in the last year or so. I didn't remember that I ever had them before, so I just thought it was weird that I saw a little boy in a park, but recently, they've advanced," I told her.

"What do you mean, advanced?" she asked.

"Well, like advanced in time. I saw Reagan as a young boy, not a baby. Now, the last few dreams and flashes I've seen, well, he's a teenager, maybe fourteen or fifteen, I guess. But, Mom, he's in trouble too," I said.

"Trouble?" she asked. I could tell this was a lot for my mom to take in too. Of course, not as much as dropping the bomb on me that I had a younger brother who was kidnapped when I was three, and it was basically my fault for distracting my dad.

"I don't know, really. But I guess now that I know he's my brother, I think, I've seen his dad's face--- or the guy who kidnapped him. I've seen him. And now in my dreams or visions, whatever, Reagan is tied up on his bed." The panic was setting in on me now. The stakes just got raised by a million because this was my brother who was being held against his will.

And I might be the one person who knows who kidnapped my brother all those years ago. I know his name too. "Mom! His name is Carl Edwards. I've seen it, that's his name. We have to tell somebody!" I shouted now, realizing what we had to do.

"Are you sure? Are you sure, Kennedy? I can't let myself go down this road again and come up empty handed, without your brother. Could you just be manifesting all these things, is that possible?" she asked. I could see in her face this was hurting her, but I was as sure as ever that my dreams were providing a guide to me. There can be no coincidence that a young boy I have dreamt about my entire life is, in fact, my brother. And now he is in danger, and I have been given the kidnapper's name.

"Mom, I have never been more sure of anything in my entire life! It can't be a coincidence. I've dreamt of him my entire life. Now I start having these dreams about Natalie, and I find her bracelet when the police couldn't find anything. And now I'm given insight into Reagan's house, and his name is Reagan, and my brother's name just happens to be the same. And the Reagan in my dream is questioning his supposed father, Carl, about whether he is his actual father, and he's writing emails to adoption agencies because he feels something is off, and now he's tied up in his room! This all has to be connected, and I'm so sure of it, Mom, I am. I know this hurts you, but what do we do now?" I asked, finally taking a breath.

"I need to call your father first, stay here," she said as she quickly left the room to grab the house phone.

I sat in my room, my heart pounding. My mind raced as to what we should do first. Do we call the police here? Do we call the Philadelphia police? What? My mom came back in the room with the phone in hand, she handed it to me.

"Hi, Dad, did you hear? I know who has Reagan. I know Reagan!" I shouted.

"Kennedy, Kennedy, stay calm, are you OK, honey? Are you sure of what you saw?" he asked me, I could hear how hesitant he was.

"Dad! I'm not going through all of this, I know Mom told you. It's him, I know it is. It all makes sense. Most of it, I still don't know how Natalie fits into this whole ordeal with Reagan, but I know it's him. I know who took him, and if you guys aren't going to do anything then I am!" I shouted, my blood starting to boil.

"Calm down, calm down, no one is saying we aren't going to do anything. It's just very hard for your mother and me, that was such a painful part of our past, and we have tried each and every day to forget and move on, because it was too much pain, Kennedy, you understand that, right? And just a name doesn't give us too much to go on. Do you have any idea where the house is? Your mother said you saw the house."

"I understand, Dad, I do, but I am so sure of this. Everything is telling me this all makes sense. We need to do something. And yes, I saw the house, I can describe it all, but I don't know where it is. I never thought about it." I suddenly realized we didn't have much to go on, and I certainly didn't want to give my parents false hope. All I knew was the name Carl Edwards. In fact, it could be a false name; he probably changed it after he kidnapped Reagan. But why did he leave Reagan's name? Did he know that was his name, or was it a mere coincidence that he picked that name? There were still a lot of holes in this story.

"OK. I believe you, Kennedy, it's no coincidence. I always thought when you were younger you might have some sort of gateway into your brother's life. You would say stuff that a normal 3-year-old wouldn't think of. I never thought you were psychic though! I'm coming up, I'm in my car now, I will meet you at the house in about four hours. Stay put and we'll decide what to do when I get there," my dad said, and then hung up the phone without waiting for me to respond.

I handed the phone back to my mom and told her what Dad had said. She agreed that we should stay here until he gets here, and then we could decide what to do. I understood where they were coming from, but how could I not try to do something now; whatever that was.

## CHAPTER 12: CARL EDWARDS

The first thing I thought to do was text Nate. I hadn't heard from him nearly all day, even after I updated him about Kyle and visiting Natalie's room. I figured his mom had probably taken his phone, being suspicious of his new UPenn friend texting him all the time. I started to text him, and oh what the hell, I dialed his number instead. It rang three times, and then he answered.

"Hello?" Nate asked.

"Nate! You will never believe this," I started.

"Oh, yeah, um, can you wait a second?" he asked. I was confused at first, but then remembered our cover plan. I waited. "Kennedy, I'm here, what's up? That was close; I was in the kitchen with my mom and dad. They still don't want me talking to you," I heard Nate say.

"Yeah, yeah, I get it. But, Nate, I have a brother!"

"A brother?" he asked, confused.

"Yes, a brother. That boy I have been dreaming about, his name is Reagan, he is my brother. We used to live in Philadelphia and he was kidnapped when I was three. It's all screwed up, and my parents like brainwashed me or something to forget, because I used to have dreams about him, but it was too painful for them to hear. That's why they divorced and my dad moved to D.C., and my mom came here," I said as quickly as I could.

"So, you have a brother? That's insane. I'm still really confused by this all. Wow. That's a lot to take in. So now what?" he asked.

"I don't know. My dad is coming up from D.C. now. And I still don't know how this all relates to Natalie. And I just started to get the hang of the dreams and flashes. I got some flashes when I was in Natalie's room earlier today," I told him again.

"Yeah, I saw your text messages. But where did it lead you?" he asked.

"Nowhere, that's the frustrating part," I told him. And then it hit me.

I told Nate to hang on, and I jumped up and flipped open my notebook that I had been recording my dreams and flashes in. I re-read one of my last entries that I wrote when I had seen Reagan. It was the picture on Carl Edwards' desk by the computer, the picture of him and Reagan. They were wearing red baseball caps, with a cursive "W" on it. Maybe it was a team that Reagan played for, and we could try and track them down that way. I told Nate what I had just remembered.

"It's probably just some little league team, that could be like trying to find a needle in a haystack," he told me. I was deflated, but I thought at least we had somewhere to start. We agreed I should tell my dad, and maybe look up some baseball hats on the Internet in the mean time. Nate said he would try and sneak out after his mom left for the gym in about an hour. I was thankful Nate was risking all this to try and help. I knew he believed me, and in me.

    I took my laptop downstairs and found my mom in the kitchen once again. I told her about the photo with the baseball caps, and she is just as sport illiterate as I am, so she offered no helpful suggestions. She agreed with Nate that searching the internet would probably not help much, but it was worth a try while we were waiting.

    I stopped only for a second to wonder again how this all related to Natalie, and then remembered what my other quest was. I was trying to identify the dad who came late on Friday night to pick someone up from the party. I had called so many people, and no one else had seen the man, or heard that anyone's dad took them home from the party early. I wanted to call the friendly policeman at the local station and remind him of that man. I told my mom my thoughts, and she said we should just wait until my dad got here.

    Since the situation on Natalie wasn't really panning out right now, I decided to search on trusty old Google to find a similar looking baseball cap. I simply typed it in: "red baseball cap with cursive "W" on it." Instantaneously, a list of hits came back. The first hit was "History of Washington D.C. professional baseball" from Wikipedia. Since it was the first hit, I clicked on it and was redirected to the Wikipedia entry. There was a picture of former President George W. Bush throwing a baseball with a Nationals jacket on. I learned that the professional baseball team in Washington D.C. was called the Washington Nationals. I tried to scan the entry quickly, and move on, and I saw something about a hat with a cursive "W" on it.

I quickly hit the back button on my browser to get back to the main Google page with the results. I checked the images page to see if I could find the hat I had seen in the picture. Sure enough, I saw the exact same cap. I clicked on the image, and below the image it said clear as day, Washington Nationals cap. I screamed!

"Mom, I think it's the Washington Nationals hat!"

"Who are they?" she asked.

"They are the professional baseball team in D.C.! Look, it's the same hat, the exact same hat!" I yelled. My mom looked over my shoulder and nodded. It wasn't as exciting to her because she hadn't seen my dream, but I was sure that it was the exact same hat. So this helped a bit. It was a Washington Nationals cap, but this could mean a lot of things. It could mean that they were at a Washington Nationals game, and they live in the area, which would be way more helpful. The problem with that was that the D.C. area is ridiculously large. They could live in D.C., or in Virginia, or even Maryland. Also, it could just mean they are fans of the team, or maybe that his favorite player is on that team. And lastly, it could still be his little league team, and they just wear those same caps.

It seems like as soon as I get a clue and get close, I have step back and realize there are about a million possibilities to every clue I think I have. My dad is a big sports fan on the other hand, so I called him quickly and relayed the information. He actually played baseball at junior college, and he always bragged about it like it was a professional contract. He verified that the Washington Nationals cap did look like what I was describing, but he also agreed that there could be a lot of possibilities as to why they were wearing it. I think he was happy though, hearing that Reagan played baseball and was a fan, because I always felt like my father was let down because I didn't enjoy sports. He always tried to get me to play catch with him when I was younger, but I couldn't have been more uninterested. He told me he was still about three hours away, but said to call him if anything else came up.

Back online, I searched for as many pictures as I could for Washington Nationals caps. I just needed to stare at the pictures. I enlarged the picture and concentrated as best I could. With a quick jolt, I received another flash.

Reagan was back on the computer in Carl's office. I could see the screen, and he was searching Google as well. He searched for his name, "Reagan Edwards." He quickly scanned the hits that popped up, but nothing interested him. His name wasn't really Reagan Edwards though, and he must have realized this, because he deleted it and typed "Patrice Edwards." I didn't know who this was, but then it was like someone was feeding me information. Reagan had always been told his mother died giving birth, her name was Patrice. If she had died, I'm sure he thought he would find an obituary, but nothing came up. I saw a blink in Reagan's eye, and he cleared the search field once again. He typed "missing children in the 1990s." Reagan was figuring it out. Tons of articles popped up, and he knew he didn't have time to go through all of them. The immensity of the entries made him so sad, I could feel it. There were so many missing kids, all in one decade. He then added a comma at the end, and put his own name in. He realized this was a long shot because if he even was a missing child, his name would most likely not really be Reagan. He did this on impulse though.

A few articles popped up, not the thousand as had before. After the first page of results, he found an article about a boy named Reagan missing from the Philadelphia area. Philadelphia was relatively close to where he lived now, so he clicked on it. Reagan scanned the article and learned a great deal. It said a 1-year-old boy named Reagan was taken from his stroller while he was in a Philadelphia mall. His father said he turned away only for a second to help his other young child, 3-year-old Kennedy, and when he turned back, Reagan was gone. Witnesses say a 30-year-old man snatched the baby and ran, but no one got a good look at him. The article reported the case was still ongoing, but it had been the one year anniversary. The article was printed in the spring of 1997.

Reagan quickly did the math. It was 2011; Reagan was now 15 years old. He was born in 1995. He would have been one year old in 1996. It fit. At the bottom of the article it said that if anyone had any information please call the Philadelphia Police, and it gave a number. Reagan quickly re-read the article, stopping on the family's names. The article said the father's name was Jack Clark, the mother Nadene, and the sister named Kennedy. He stared at the name Kennedy, my name! He fixated on it. He felt something when he looked at my name. I could feel it in him through my flash. He was aware of what was going on. I felt warm. He knew this was him.

He grabbed for his cell phone, but he had left it in his room. He took a piece of paper and wrote down the number for the Philadelphia PD. He then wrote down my name, Kennedy, with a star next to it. I knew he felt some sort of connection to me, like I always had felt with him. Just then, Carl came through the office door and startled Reagan. Reagan instinctively tried to minimize the computer screen window he had up, and shoved the paper into his pocket. He succeeded in closing the computer window, but as he reached for the piece of paper, Carl dove on top of him and grabbed it.

My eyes flung open, and my mother was staring wide eyed at me. I didn't have time to explain everything to her, and I jumped up and ran to my notebook. I couldn't stop recording all the details now!

My mom followed me, and I explained what I had just seen. If my mom ever doubted what I was telling her she definitely believed me now. She was surprised at how detailed a vision I'd had right in front of her.

"Can you make yourself have these visions?" she asked me.

"I'm trying to. I think I'm getting better at it, now that I'm aware that I can have them at all, but it doesn't always just work that way. I can't control what I'm going to see, but I've kind of figured out triggers," I told her.

"Triggers?" she asked.

"Yeah, kind of like some connection to the person. In Natalie's room I touched a picture of her when she got all that hair cut off, remember? And it triggered me seeing her now when she was playing with her hair," I told her.

"Oh."

"Yeah," I responded back.

I furiously scribbled down the summary of the story of my brother, Reagan, and then about the Washington Nationals baseball cap. I realized my computer was still downstairs, and I scurried back down. My mother followed me like a lost puppy. I couldn't worry about her right now though, because I was too focused on what was running through my mind.

I plopped down on the chair at the kitchen table and began googling again. I figured the next step would be to try and find an address for Carl Edwards, even though that sounded like a common enough name, and also because he most likely changed his name when he snatched my baby brother. I started off with "Carl Edwards" in the search field. I should have learned the lesson from Reagan's searching and narrowed the city down, so I corrected my error. I typed in "Carl Edwards, Philadelphia, PA." Again, a number of hits came back, including a NASCAR driver named Carl Edwards who had some connection to Pennsylvania. I tried to read the little blurb about each hit, trying not to waste time. Nothing stood out to me, and I returned to try and narrow the search down again. I couldn't think of another clue to add to my search bar. I quickly deleted "Philadelphia, PA" in the search box, and meant to delete "Carl Edwards" too, but my fingers got ahead of my brain. I typed in "young boy missing" behind "Carl Edwards," so the search bar read, "Carl Edwards, young boy missing." I realized my mistake as soon as my pinky finger hit the enter bar, but the search results had already popped up on my screen.

## CHAPTER 13:

## PHILADELPHIA PD

The article that was the first hit to pop up in Google drew me in. The blurb on the front screen said, "Young Boy Killed by Father's Firearm." It sounded too tragically terrible, but I had to click on it. The story that followed, read:

*Young Boy Killed by Father's Firearm*

*Father Member of Philadelphia P.D.*

*Yesterday was a tragic day in Philadelphia, especially for one specific family. Their 3-year-old son, Reagan, was killed when he accidentally shot himself with his father's firearm. Carl Edwards, an honorable member of the Philadelphia Police Department, could not be reached for a comment, but it is being reported that Edwards left his firearm out, and loaded, only for a few brief minutes, but the rambunctious 3-year-old stumbled upon the deadly mistake.*

*Officer Edwards, like all members of the police department, sometimes had his firearm at home with him, but we were told he is very careful with storing his firearm immediately when he is home and off duty.*

*A close friend of the family has told us that Edwards has a safe that he locks his firearm in, and puts it on a high shelf in his closet. He started the practice when Reagan was born three years earlier.*

*It was a terribly sad scene at the Edwards household as Carl himself heard the shot and found his young son lifeless. Reagan will be remembered as a curious, intelligent child, and he will be dearly missed by his family and neighbors who enjoyed watching the young boy play out in the street with other children. Carl Edwards and his wife Nancy do not have any other children.*

*Reagan will have a private funeral with family and close friends only.*

My eyes were pouring out tears by the time I finished. I almost didn't even realize there was a picture of Carl Edwards at the very bottom, in his police uniform. It was the same man I saw in my dreams and visions with Reagan. It was the same man in the picture with Reagan on the desk in the office. My mom had wandered over behind me again at some point, and I just stared at the computer. This all made so much more sense now. Poor Carl Edwards.

"That poor guy," I said aloud.

"What do you mean?" my mother said defensively. "He kidnapped your little brother. The hell with him!" she screamed.

I didn't mean to upset her. I could only imagine how difficult this was on her. I tried to calm her down and explain. "I didn't mean it like that, he was still wrong. But it makes sense," I said.

"How?" she asked defiantly again.

"He lost his son in a tragic accident, it was his fault, but it was a mistake. His son's name was Reagan, what are the odds?" I told her.

"So?" she prodded.

"So, I mean imagine what he was going through, you and Dad were absolutely devastated," I started to get out, but then she interrupted me.

"Destroyed is more accurate," she said.

"You and Dad were destroyed, and it wasn't either of your faults, it was mine, and this guy Carl, it was his fault, he left his gun out, and his son died. How terrible he must he have felt? His poor wife. It makes sense why I always thought that Reagan was fine. I can tell that Carl really loved our Reagan. He obviously sounds crazy, but he loved Reagan, and he treated him well, until now when he tied him up obviously," I told her.

"Honey, you are wrong. It was not your fault. How could you think that?" she only responded to one little part of what I had just said. I was quiet.

"It was, Mom. If I wasn't climbing in that candy store, Dad wouldn't have been distracted, and Carl wouldn't have been able to take Reagan, but I know it's more important that we find him now."

"It was NOT your fault. I don't want to hear you ever say that again, Kennedy, ever!" she demanded.

I still believed it was my fault, but there was nothing I could do just talking about it, we needed to act. Now that the entire mess was making more sense to me, we still didn't have an address for Carl Edwards. I knew he was once a Philadelphia police officer, but did he still live there? I must have looked confused, because my mom spoke up.

"What about calling the Philadelphia Police Department?" she asked.

"Actually, that's not a bad idea. What should we say though?" I asked back, impressed at my mom's intuition as to what I was thinking.

"Well, we could say we were old neighbors of the Edwards, and wondered if they had a forwarding address for Carl," she suggested. That was a good idea, but what if he still lived in Philadelphia and worked for the Philadelphia P.D., then we'd look like idiots. It was worth a shot, though.

"We can try, keep your fingers crossed," I said. I picked up my cell phone, but my mom stopped me.

"I'll call from the house. It will sound better if I talk," she said. She had a point.

She grabbed the downstairs phone and we looked up the number for the Philadelphia Police Department. My mom dialed and it seemed like it was taking forever for the ten numbers to be punched. I heard someone pick up, and my mom began talking. She went with the neighbor story, and she sounded cool and calm. I gave her a lot of credit. She had gone through a lot today, but she was really coming through. It looks like I'm not the only one in the family with a wanna-be detective spirit.

She was put on hold, and told me that the receptionist was new, and didn't have anything in the system, but after my mom told her it had been almost fifteen years ago, she said she would ask some of the older guys in the office.

I scooched closer to my mom to try to hear what was being said. I couldn't make it all out, but I did hear something about an officer knowing Carl, and his wife had his address at home, but they really weren't allowed to give out such personal information. My mom then used her sweetest mother voice to coax it out of her. The receptionist said she would do her best and call her back. Apparently, Carl's old partner still worked there, was about to retire, and he tried to keep in touch with his old friend.

The phone rang a few minutes later, and it was the receptionist. My mom began writing on a nearby kitchen tablet, and I heard her say, "Thank you so much, you have no idea." The lady really did have no idea how much she has helped even though they were breaking the rules. I realized the irony that the Philadelphia police had never been able to find my brother, until we called them some fourteen years later to get a man's address who worked for them.

My mom turned the tablet toward me so I could see the address without saying a word. She picked up the phone again, and I heard her say to my dad, "Jack, where are you? Reagan's in D.C. Our boy is in a house a few minutes away from where you and Janet live. Jack, do you hear me?"

I could not believe that my brother was only a few minutes away from my dad in D.C. I wonder how long he has been there. That didn't matter now though. My mom handed me the phone.

"Kennedy, I'm only a few minutes away, sit tight," and he hung up.

I really could not believe everything that had transpired. I tried to think about what my dad would want to do once he arrived. Would he want to call the Pittsburgh police, or the Philadelphia police, or the D.C. police?

Natalie. I had forgotten about her for a few hours while we were on the hunt to find Reagan and Carl Edwards. Now that we had solved the mystery about this little boy I had always dreamed about, and where he was now, I still didn't understand how Natalie fit into all of this. There had to be some kind of connection, or trigger, between the two of them since they would come to me in my dreams back to back since the night of Natalie's disappearance.

As if on cue, my cell began to ring, and it was Nate. "Kennedy, anything new?" he asked eagerly. I recounted all the details and he told me how he tried to sneak out and come over like he said he would, hours ago, but his mom caught him. He told her the truth, the whole truth, and she seemed sympathetic to the dreams and visions I was having. He told her about Reagan, and she began to cry. No one could really doubt me after revealing I had a brother who I had always dreamt about. That was my trump card, and it worked on Nate's mother. She felt so bad for my parents, and now for me, and she told Nate he could talk to me again. He wanted to do more than that, he wanted to come over now.

"Yeah, sure. Come over. My dad's almost here," I told him.

My mom seemed to be taking in everything much better now after her cool phone call and getting Carl's address. She pulled out a pitcher of lemonade and poured us both a glass. I told her Nate was coming over now, so she poured him a glass as well. Thank God for manners. Nate was here in what seemed like seconds, and a few minutes later my dad walked in the front door.

He ran right to my mother and gave her the biggest hug I have ever seen. It was very weird seeing them embrace like that, and show affection, because I had never seen my parents touch each other at all, ever. They were divorced for as long as I could remember, thanks to that crackpot hypnotist and psychiatrist I saw after Reagan was kidnapped by Carl. They held on to each other for a few minutes as Nate and I watched close by. After they were done, he came to me and gave me a hug and a kiss on my cheek.

"Kennedy, you are amazing, you know that, right? You did this, all of this," he told me.

I kind of blushed. My dad was so proud of me. It was a good feeling. My dad has told me that he was proud of me before- I got good grades, I was a good kid, didn't drink, didn't get in trouble at school, you know, the normal stuff- but this was different. He glowed.

"But what do we do now?" I asked, being pulled back into reality that Reagan was not with us and he was in some kind of danger.

"We call the D.C. police," my mother interjected.

"No, I'm going myself, give me the address," my father demanded. I could see him looking around for a sheet of paper with the address on it.

"I'm going with you," I said quickly.

"Me too," Nate spoke up.

"No one is going anywhere, we are going to let the police handle this," my mom was back in the conversation, and she was determined to get her way, I could tell.

"Hell no we are not. They did nothing back then, and they aren't doing shit with Natalie, I am going and getting our son back. This ends tonight," my dad said with force.

My mom made a little "humph" noise as she was obviously defeated and there was no way of stopping my determined father. I craved his eye contact so he could agree that I was going with him.

"You are staying with your mother, and that's final," he looked back at me.

"That's final? I don't think so. I'm the one who found him, practically, plus you might need me," I pleaded.

I had made a valid point and I could see my dad considering the option. My mom spoke up again. "You are not going with him, Kennedy, we have no idea how unstable this Carl man is, and obviously something is wrong with him because after all these years he has tied Reagan up."

"Your mom's right, Kennedy. You have done a great job, kiddo, but I can't risk losing you too," he looked sad again, like the past had just come back and slapped him in the face.

"Dad, he is confused. He caught Reagan on the computer while he was putting it together who he was- who we were. He wrote my name down on a piece of paper. Carl was threatened, he's just scared," I told him.

"You're probably right, but there's nothing more dangerous than a man who has everything to lose, and is scared out of his mind," my dad said aloud.

No one spoke for a few seconds. I knew my dad was right. I knew that Carl had really loved Reagan, and it made sense to me. He probably had something wrong with him, and he may have even thought that our Reagan was really his Reagan, his son, and that's why he treated him so well all these years, but now that Reagan had started to put it all together, he freaked out. I get it. But my dad needed me.

"Dad, I understand. I will be so careful, even stay in the car, but I might get a flash, or vision, or whatever you want to call it, and it may help you. Please," I told him. I think he could tell I was being so genuinely sincere, and he finally broke.

"OK, let me go to the bathroom real quick, grab a couple sodas for the road, and we're leaving in two minutes. I'm sorry, Nadene," he said as he looked back to my mom.

With that, my dad walked into the hallway bathroom. My mom opened up the refrigerator to pull out some drinks according to my dad's instructions. I frantically looked around for my notebook with all of my dream summaries and my cell phone. I was looking around like I needed to grab something else, but what I needed was not a something, it was a someone.

Nate was looking straight at me. He whispered, "And me?"

"Nate, you should just stay here with my mom and your parents," I tried to tell him.

"I want to be there for you guys. I'll stay in the car with you. I've been kind of like your sidekick this whole time, don't bench me now, Coach." It was his weak attempt at a sports analogy, but I appreciated the effort.

"Call your parents," I told him, then headed to the bathroom door. "Listen Dad, Nate is coming, but he'll stay in the car with me. He's been the only one who has really believed me this whole time, I need him."

"OK. In the car now," he replied. He walked by me, grabbed the drinks from my mom, kissed her on the cheek, freaking me out yet again, and out the front door to his SUV. Nate and I followed him quickly. I turned around, "Bye, Mom. I love you." Her eyes were filled with tears already, and I couldn't tell if she was worried about us, or so happy that her baby boy might be returning tonight. It was probably both. She just smiled and nodded her head, which I understood as an "I love you" back.

I ran to catch up with Nate and my dad and jumped into the SUV. "Did you call your parents?" I asked Nate.

"Yes," he said. "My mom's coming over to be with your mom." That may be the nicest thing anyone in this community has ever done for my mom, and I was appreciative of the gesture of kindness.

# CHAPTER 14:

# ANTICIPATION RISING

The car ride back to D.C. should only have taken about four hours, and even less with the way my dad was driving. He made it in less than four hours back up to Pittsburgh this morning driving like a mad man, I assume. No one really said a word for a long time. The sun was still out and bright until the mid afternoon slowly turned to night. My dad knew the route well, and the address where Carl Edwards supposedly now lived was literally only ten minutes away from where my dad lives. Actually, it was in the same school district. His stepchildren were older, and weren't in high school anymore, so they wouldn't know Reagan. How crazy would that have been though?

We started to get close, and I realized we didn't have a plan. "So, what's the plan, Dad?" I asked. My dad was uber concentrated on the road ahead. I had to repeat myself, "Dad, what's the plan for when we actually get there? What are we going to do?"

"You mean, what am I going to do," he corrected me.

"Sure, you," I gave in.

"I'm not sure. I'm going to go and knock on the door, make sure it's the right house," he said, still concentrated on the road.

"OK, but then what? What if it is Carl's house?" I kept at it.

"I'm not sure, Kennedy, I just need to worry about getting your brother, that's all." I knew he realized it wasn't that simple, but I think he might have been just a little afraid, and rightfully so. We really had no idea if Carl would be there, if he is crazy, if he'd come at him with a weapon, or what.

"Well, why don't we come up with some kind of a story? What about saying you're a college scout for baseball or something? Would that work? I mean, he definitely plays baseball, so that could work, right?" I asked. I was proud of myself for coming up with an idea so quickly.

"I guess. Or I could just tell him I'm Reagan's father and I'm taking him home now."

"Dad! No you can't!" I yelled.

He turned to me for the first time all trip and smiled. "I know, Kennedy. I'm a college scout, that works, OK?" It worked for me. It would be a good chance to make Carl be polite to him, and not slam the door, or punch him in the face.

We had an idea, but then I began to worry that my dad didn't have anything to defend himself with. We should only have been about twenty minutes away, but just ahead we saw a massive amount of traffic. My dad groaned.

"What's going on?" Nate asked from the back seat.

"D.C. rush hour traffic," my dad said. It was 6 p.m. on a weekday so of course there was traffic, especially in D.C. This totally ruined our momentum. We were only minutes away from my little brother who was tied up by a scared psychopath, and we were in bumper-to-bumper traffic. My dad honked his horn, tried to ride up the side of the road, and did every trick in the book, but we were going nowhere.

The anticipation was almost unbearable. At one point I thought of asking if we could just leave the car and run, but then I realized that twenty minutes in a car was not the same as twenty minutes of running; plus I couldn't run twenty minutes if my life depended on it. I may be able to run twenty minutes if my brother's life depended on it though, which it just might. Nonetheless, it would take forever to get out and run, and that was not an option.

We really had no option but to sit in the car and wait it out. I could tell my dad was getting increasingly antsy, and every time I tried to ask him about when we got to Reagan's house, he shut me down. Nate knew enough to stay quiet in the back. My dad's cell phone rang. It was my mom.

"Here, you talk to her, I can't right now," he said, handing me the phone.

"Hi, Mom," I said, trying to sound cheery, but normal.

"What's going on, where are you guys now?" she asked.

"Well, we're close, but we're sitting in traffic, not moving at all."

"Oh dear! Is your father going nuts?" she asked.

"Of course," I said, trying to keep my voice low so I didn't distract my dad, I could tell he was not taking waiting very well.

"Do you have a plan for when you arrive at the house?" my mom broke the silence.

"Yeah, kind of," I started to say, and my mom interrupted me.

"Kind of? You put your father on the phone right now!" she demanded.

I looked at my dad, and he shook his head. "Mom, it's OK, we've gotta go, we've got it under control, we will call you the minute we get there, OK?" I asked, hoping she would understand. There was silence on the other end, and then I heard Nate's mom's voice in the background. "I'm sure they will be fine, Nadene, let's get a cup of coffee."

I was so thankful that Nate's mom was there, my mom really needed someone with her right now, if only to calm her down. With that, my mom agreed, and said goodbye.

The minutes seemed to tick by one by one, painfully slow. One minute I looked at the clock on the dash and it was 6:30, and what seemed like hours later it was 6:45. We were starting to slowly move by 7:15 p.m., but it was more of a crawl really. The forward motion helped ease everyone's nerves though, because at least we were physically making progress and no longer at a complete stand still. 7:30 came and went, then 7:45 and 8:00. I could see the traffic starting to lighten up as we neared the end of normal rush hour traffic, but D.C. traffic was a monster of its own. My mom called again, but my dad answered this time.

"Nadene, we are not there yet, we're sitting in god damn traffic!" he yelled. I grabbed the phone from him.

"Mom, sorry, we're still in traffic, I promised you we'd call OK, it's not helping you calling every hour, OK?" I told her, hoping she'd understand.

"OK, Kennedy, just be safe, please, all of you. I still think we should call the cops."

"Mom, no." I was firm.

"OK, bye honey, call me soon," she said.

The more my mom worried, the more I worried, and I started to wonder if we should call the cops. I didn't want to bring it up aloud, so I texted Nate what I was feeling. He agreed he was getting nervous too, but he knew my dad would never go for us calling the police. I racked my brain for another solution, but could come up with nothing. My dad didn't even notice that our phones were dinging with incoming text messages back and forth. He was too concentrated on the slow moving traffic. We took a few minutes to try and think of how we could involve the cops without being too premature, or letting my dad know. We had some time due to the traffic, so we brainstormed. Nate asked if we could call ahead and tell them to come in 15 minutes, or something to that extent. I told him I didn't think it worked like restaurant reservations, so no. I then thought that maybe once we got closer and knew how many minutes away from the house we were, that we could call my mom and tell her to call in x amount of minutes. Nate didn't think this would work because my mom would get too nervous, probably call early, and tell them something she didn't need to. I agreed with him.

It was now 8:30 p.m. and we could see the road opening up ahead. After nearly two hours of not being able to move in traffic, I saw my dad's hands tighten on the steering wheel. He hadn't talked in an hour. I texted Nate back, telling him that when we get there, he should stay in the car and after two minutes or so, if we weren't out of the house, he should call 9-1-1. He thought this was our best option too, even though it was risky. We had no idea what we were going to be walking into at Carl Edwards' house. Two minutes might be two minutes too late, but it could also be premature if we haven't made our way up to Reagan's room.

The summer night started taking over the daylight. If you had to classify it, I'd say it was early dusk. It was too light to be dusk, but it was definitely no longer daytime.

My dad made quick time once the traffic cleared. He was zipping back and forth between lanes, and when we exited off the highway, I knew we were nearing the house. I had been nervous since the moment we decided to come down to get Reagan, but now that we were only minutes away, after waiting so long in traffic, I really got butterflies. I suddenly felt stupid for not trying to have any more visions on our way down, not that I knew what I was looking for. I squeezed my eyes shut, hoping something useful would flash up, but it didn't. My dad must have seen this, because he reached over and touched my hand.

"It'll be OK, Kennedy, I promise," he spoke for the first time in many minutes.

"Thanks, Dad, I know. Are we close?" I asked, knowing we must be.

"Yes. Maybe five minutes." I looked back at Nate, making sure he knew how close we were too. He had heard what my dad said, and he was inching up on the edge of his seat. In less than the five projected minutes we were pulling up on Reagan's street. It seemed like a very nice neighborhood not much different than the one Nate and I lived in. The houses were comparably big, with lots of grass out front and in the back, from what we could see from the road.

There was no one on the street, as dusk turned into night. My dad slowed the car as he was looking at house numbers. We slowed to a stop out front of a large brick house. I thought I might recognize it, but in all of my dreams and visions I had never seen outside of the house. I knew the landscape of the inside, but didn't recognize this house, although it was large, and seemed uninviting somehow. I was silently telling myself that everything would be OK as I went to reach for the door handle to open the car door.

"What are you doing?" my dad yelped.

"Getting out, why?" I asked.

"No, you are not. You both are staying put in this car, if I need you, I'll call you," he said with no hint of hesitation or negotiation in his voice.

"Dad, you are not going in there alone, plus I know what the house looks like, I know what Carl looks like, I need to help." There was zero chance I was waiting in this car. I figured Nate would be stationed here, and that would work well with our plan, but I couldn't let my dad go in alone, no way.

"Kennedy, this is not the time to do this. We are wasting time, and he might see us out here, you are staying here. That's it," he said, as he opened up his center console and grabbed what looked like a lead pipe. He started to get out of his driver's seat. He glanced back to Nate, "Nate, stay here, watch my daughter, and if I'm not out in five minutes, call the cops." It looks like my dad had the same idea as us, except that he didn't understand I was coming with him.

My dad exited the car, and so did I. I met him around the backside of the SUV. I started in a low voice, watching my tone, "Dad, listen, I understand, but I know where Reagan's room is, I can help you. Is that a pipe?" I asked, gesturing to the object in his hand.

My dad interrupted, "Don't worry about what it is, it's just in case I need it to defend myself. And you're still not going in there with me, just tell me where Reagan's room is."

"It's upstairs, but that's beside the point, let me come with you, I need to," I begged of him.

My dad looked around. I know he was trying to figure out another plan that didn't involve me going up to the front door with him. "How about I go to the front door, knock, speak to Carl, and see how it goes. Why don't you walk around back? Can you see Reagan's room from the back? Have you seen that?"

"Actually, yes. He threw a baseball through his window at some point, so yes, you can see his room from the back yard," I told him.

"OK then. You go around back. You have your cell phone, yes? If anything happens, call me, or call Nate, or the police. OK?" my dad said.

"It's a plan. Be careful, Dad," I told him.

"You too, Kennedy. Let's go get your brother back." With that, he started walking up the front lawn to the door. There was one single light overhead the front door. There were no other lights on in the house that we could see from the lawn. I started to make my way around the side path of the house. There was a wooden gate as I neared the back that I easily slid open. I had never seen this side of the house before. I debated on leaving the gate open or closed, and decided to keep it open. I took one glance back at Nate who was standing outside of the car, scanning between the front door and where I was standing. There was definitely no turning back now.

## CHAPTER 15: PLUS ONE

    I twirled back around and headed further into the back yard of Carl Edwards' home. I had planned to walk toward the middle and look up to see if I could see into Reagan's room, but as I got into the back yard, I saw a shed in the back right corner. It was the same shed that I had seen Reagan staring out at through his bedroom window. For some reason, I was drawn to it. There were no lights on in the back yard, so I slowly inched my way closer to the shed. It was a small, wooden shed that looked pretty worn down. It piqued my curiosity. The wood was discolored and there were some branches resting on the top from the tree that hung overhead. It had definitely seen better days. There was a metal baseball bat resting against the outside, next to the door. Reagan did play baseball after all, so this wasn't too conspicuous. It only meant that we were at the right house. This made me look over to my left and scan the yard a little better. There were baseballs strewn all over the yard, with a large net that I guessed was for Reagan to throw the ball off of. This was definitely the right house.

Then I turned back to the shed, and I swore I heard a noise. I can't really describe it, it wasn't someone talking, it wasn't even necessarily movement, but I heard something. I tried to open the door of the shed, but there was a large silver lock on it. "Hello?" I said into the shed as I shoved my eye against the small separation between wooden planks on the front of the shed.

I heard nothing. I strained my eye as I tried to look into the darkness of the shed, but I couldn't make out anything. I fiddled with the lock, but it was obvious that I needed a key. I could no longer hear any noises, so I started to turn around to catch a glimpse of Reagan's room, and just as I turned, I heard it. "Help." That was all. It was quiet, and weak, but it was definitely someone's voice.

"Is somebody in there? Hello? Are you in the shed?" I asked quietly as not to cause any distraction for my dad dealing with Carl in the house. I started to panic. Was Reagan stuck in this shed? Was he so weak, or hurt, that he could barely make out a four-letter word? I tugged at the lock, trying to separate the piece that held it together, but I was no match for it. I reached for my phone to call Nate to come help, but I felt a hand on my shoulder and I jumped.

"Kennedy," Nate said. He was the one behind me.

"Thank God! Someone's in there. I think Reagan's in here, help me get this open," I pleaded as I pulled with all my might against the lock.

"It's a metal lock, is there a key anywhere?" he asked. He was now starting to sweat and his hands were shaking.

"No, no, I haven't found one. Wait, did you call the police? Has it been two minutes? Is my dad OK?" I asked, suddenly remembering that my father is probably face to face with Carl Edwards right now. We both stopped, trying to see if we heard anything from inside the house, but we didn't.

I grabbed the bat resting on the shed and lifted it above my head. Nate grabbed my arm to stop my swing. He turned over a nearby pot in a last ditch effort to find a key to quietly open the lock. He found nothing. As he was standing up his eyes darted to something, and reached for it alongside the shed nearest the fence. We both heard, "Help!" a little stronger this time. It didn't sound like a teenage boy's voice though.

"Reagan?" Nate asked. He must have been thinking the same thing as me. There was no response. "Reagan, is that you?" Nate asked again.

"Natalie," the voice from inside spoke. We both froze. Nate and I looked at each other, trying to process if we both just heard the same thing. I slowly swallowed and turned back to the shed.

"Natalie?" I asked, hesitantly. I really thought my mind was playing tricks on me, but Nate didn't seem to disagree with what I had heard.

"Yes. Natalie. Who's there? Who's out there?" she asked frantically.

My heart started racing and Nate fumbled with what I now saw was a key that he had reached for by the side of the fence. He tried to put it into the lock. I flung the door open and had to squint to see Natalie, my best friend, curled up in the fetal position. Her blonde hair was dark and greasy, and she looked so tiny in that dark corner. I started to walk in when I heard a loud shot!

My dad. I turned to Nate who had heard the shot as well. "You stay with Natalie," I screamed to Nate as I ran to the back door only a few feet away. The kitchen light was on, but I couldn't see any movement. I touched the kitchen door and my eyes banged together. I was having another flash. I saw Reagan in his room, rocking back and forth in his bed. His head was turning from side to side as he tried to wiggle the tape off his mouth. With a small crack, Reagan fell forward onto his bed. His arms had been taped behind his back and he must have broken through. He pulled his arms around and peeled the tape off of his bound legs. He tried to stand up quickly, but was very unstable and toppled back onto his bed. I could see in his face that he had urgency on his mind as he pushed himself to get up. The flash ended.

"Reagan? Reagan, can you hear me?" I shouted upward, hoping he could hear me if he was still in his room. I was sure that what I had just seen was happening in real time. Reagan was breaking free and trying to leave his room. "Reagan? Can you hear me?" I shouted again. I heard no response. I ran around to the front of the house and saw that the front door was open. I was still worried and thinking about Natalie, but Nate was with her. I really hoped he had called the cops. Natalie needed medical attention, I'm sure, and if that shot connected with somebody, they would definitely need medical attention.

There was a light on in the foyer, and I recognized the house as soon as I stepped in. I was walking slower now because I hadn't heard any movement or noise since that shot a minute ago. I thought I heard something upstairs, and I shouted for Reagan again. There was still no response, but I could feel him. I suddenly got very tired, like my body weighed a thousand pounds. I felt unsteady, and my body swayed left to right with each step I took inside. I was feeling what Reagan was feeling, I thought. I saw the office to my right. The door was shut. I saw the living room next to the kitchen, and the couch I had once seen Reagan sitting on, before he knew that his entire world had been a lie, before he knew for sure that the man he had been calling Dad all his life was not his father. I stumbled step by step into the kitchen that was fully lit. I could see into the back yard and I saw Nate and Natalie out by the shed, but the light stung my eyes like they were not used to the brightness. My stomach grumbled, but I walked on. I spun around in the kitchen, seeing no one, and then I saw a door to my left, next to the refrigerator, that was wide open. The door led to the garage, and I saw a black car parked inside, but it was what was in front of the car that immediately caught my attention.

My father was on the ground, his face toward me as I quickly put together what had happened. My father had been on the receiving end of that shot I had heard minutes ago. His face was pale and his eyes soft. They opened wider as I stepped closer. A stream of tears seemed stagnant on his lower lids. I really was not even thinking about the fact that Carl Edwards could be inside the garage with the loaded gun, I just needed to get to my dad and help him.

He tried to pull himself up the single stair that connected the garage to the kitchen as I approached. "Kennedy, no!" he said using all of the strength he had left. I couldn't even push any words out of my mouth asking if he was OK, or if Carl was nearby. I got to him and knelt down, holding his head in my hands.

"Dad," was all I could get out. He just stared up at me, and I thought this would be the last time I would see my dad alive. I could see him fading away.

"So you are Kennedy," I heard a voice say, and I quickly jolted my head up to see Carl Edwards emerge from the back of the garage. He had the gun in his hand tapping it against the side of his thigh as he walked toward us, kicking away my dad's lead pipe to the side. I stayed kneeling next to my dad as I watched this man come right at us with the gun. I didn't respond to him. "I've been looking for you, but your dad found me first," he said as he pointed the gun toward my dad's body. I looked down into my dad's eyes and they were shutting slowly.

"Dad, stay with me, please. Please!" I shook him as I said this.

"I'm sorry," was all he could get out.

"Yeah, I'm sorry too, I never thought it would come to this," Carl said, now standing just a foot away from us. I didn't even know how to respond to him, the man just shot my father. I had never been one to not be able to quickly respond, but a lot had just hit me in the past five minutes. I still felt weak and my arms were shaking as I was trying to hold my dad's head steady in my hands. I had to lower them, and place his head on the step in front of me. I kept my arm resting on his shoulder though. I could feel him breathing, ever so lightly, but it was still a good sign.

"Why did you do this?" I asked Carl as I looked him straight in the eye.

"Why? Why? Because he was trying to take my son!" he said angrily. I could see his hand with the gun in it shaking back and forth, and his head was twitching every few seconds. This was not a good sign. I had to push the issue though.

"Your son? Reagan? He's not your son, he's his son," I said pointing to my dad. I knew this would set him off, but I was angry now. This guy was honestly saying he shot my dad because he was trying to take *his* son!

"Reagan is my son!" he yelled back, still shaking.

"No, he's not. You are not his father! And why would you tie him up and lock him in his room?" I said with indignation.

Carl Edwards was shaking his head back and forth and mumbling to himself now. He hit the side of his head with his gun, as if trying to settle his mind down. He took a deep breath, lowered his gun and stared back at me. "How did you know Reagan's tied up? How did you know?" he demanded.

"I just did, but he's not anymore, and the police are on their way," I said, trying to sound convincing, and although I hoped the police were on their way, I didn't know for sure that they were.

"The police? No. The police aren't coming. No." Carl was mumbling heavily now, and I tried to think if it would be wise to try and drag my dad into the house while Carl seemed distracted. I popped up and grabbed my dad's shirt by his shoulders and tried to pull him in. I got him halfway in the kitchen door before Carl noticed.

"Stop!" he said as he pointed the gun right at me now. "Stop right there."

"OK. OK. I stopped, put the gun down, Carl," I said trying to stay calm.

"How do you know my name? How did *he* know my name?" he asked, referring to my dad. I didn't know what to say. I froze. My legs felt weak and unstable. "How do you know who I am?" Carl yelled loudly. I was hoping Nate had called the cops, I was praying with every ounce of faith in my body that the police were close, because it seemed like everything I said set Carl off, and now the gun was pointed straight on me.

I stuttered trying to think of how to respond. I felt like someone pushed my shoulders straight down, forcing me down on top of my dad. I collapsed on him.

"I can't let you go. You know too much. Both of you know too much," I heard Carl say as he lowered the gun to where I now lie on the floor. "You know too much." Then a loud bang echoed through the house, making my bones shiver.

I shut my eyes and tried to cover my dad. My body was tense, and I was using every bit of muscle I had left to brace for the impending impact of the bullet Carl just shot. I was still covering my dad with my own head facing back in toward the kitchen, and I heard a thump. I didn't feel like I had been shot. I felt like a failure, Carl must have shot my father again. I couldn't live if this were true. My dad was barely breathing as it is.

I slowly opened up my eyes and I saw him. For the first time in real life, since I was three years old, I saw Reagan. He was standing about ten feet away in the middle of the kitchen, gun raised. He looked exhausted, and could barely stand up straight. I jumped up and turned around to see Carl lying lifeless on the ground a foot away. His face was staring right at my dad's body, his eyes still open. I picked up Carl's gun, just in case he was not dead, but all signs indicated that he was. Reagan had hit him right in the chest and blood was spilling out all over the floor. I dragged my dad the rest of the way into the kitchen, hoping to keep him from getting more of Carl's blood on his legs.

I knelt down to listen to his chest, but his breaths were shallow. I looked back to Reagan and he was sitting at the kitchen table, trying desperately to keep from falling over. "Are you OK, Reagan?" I asked him. I forgot for a moment that he wouldn't know who I was, some stranger with another stranger on the floor of his kitchen.

"Are you Kennedy?" he asked.

"Yes. I'm your sister."

"Hi," he said with the biggest smile he could conjure up.

"Hi," I said back. I got caught up staring at him. He looked so familiar, and it almost felt like we had been brother and sister for fifteen years, not for the short period we actually had seen each other. Then we heard the police.

"Police! Who's in here? Hands up!" I heard them yelling.

"We're in here, help!" I yelled back. Someone needed to help my dad, and fast.

"Police! Hands up! Hands up!" they yelled, as a bunch of policemen, all in black, came running into the kitchen. My hands were in the air, and I could see Reagan trying to lift his hands, but couldn't.

"Gun! He's got a gun!" I heard one policeman say. He threw Reagan to the ground, shoving the gun from the table down to the ground.

"He didn't do anything. He's weak. That man had him tied up in his room for days. Don't hurt him!" I shouted. They were after the wrong guy. "Don't hurt him, that's my brother!" I yelled. "And this is my dad, he's shot, I don't know where, help, please!" At this, a few police broke off and came to assess my dad. One went to Carl, and I heard him say he was dead. Then one checked my father.

"He's breathing, but it's shallow. He's shot in the shoulder, he's lost a lot of blood, and he needs to get to a hospital now." I was so scared for my dad. He had been bleeding for quite some time now, I hadn't realized that the blood on his leg was not from Carl, but was his own.

The police quickly realized Reagan was not at fault, and helped him up. The ambulance arrived and the paramedics came storming into the kitchen. They hoisted my dad up on the gurney and out he went. They asked me to quickly tell them what had happened. I told them that my dad was shot, and this guy Carl had shot him. He had kidnapped my brother, Reagan, years ago, and we came back to get him. The policeman was looking at me like I was a complete lunatic.

The paramedics tried to get Reagan to go on a gurney too, but he said he was fine. The weakness and fatigue that had plagued me just minutes before had left my body. My mind was still spinning trying to comprehend everything that had transpired, but physically I felt better. I walked over to Reagan and in typical big sister mode, I told him he had better go get checked out. He just smiled at me and walked outside with the paramedics. Two of them were on either side of him, still helping him support his own weight.

Cops were all over, taking pictures, asking for more information on what had happened, and just generally getting in my way. I needed to see how my dad was, and I needed to find Natalie and Nate.

I walked out the front door and saw Nate standing behind an ambulance. I ran over. "How is she?" I asked him.

"Natalie? She's good, surprisingly. They said she's severely dehydrated, and she's a little out of it, and light hurts her eyes, but she's good they said."

"Thank God!" I said as I pushed past Nate. I had to see my best friend. "Natalie!" I yelled as I approached her in the back of the ambulance. She was sitting in the back with an IV in her arm.

"Kennedy! I can't believe it's you guys. I can't believe it," she said in a slightly crackly voice. She kept shaking her head slightly.

"Nat, I'm so happy you're OK. How did you end up here? Did Nate tell you that I have a brother? I'm going to call your parents right now," I said. I don't know where I thought of that, with the million things going through my mind, but they likely hadn't been told their daughter was found yet.

"Thanks, Kennedy, for everything, you have no idea how thankful I am," she smiled. A paramedic looked at me and told me that they were taking her to the closest hospital, and my dad would go there too. They said I could ride with whichever ambulance I wanted.

"I'll go with Natalie, you go with your dad," Nate stepped up into the ambulance.

"OK, good. Call your parents too, Nate. I'll call my mom and Mrs. Hall," I told him, just as they shut the ambulance doors on Natalie and Nate. I scrambled backward and ran to the other ambulance, holding my father. I realized how lucky we were that they had two ambulances there instead of just one. My dad was still on the gurney, but it hadn't been lifted up into the back of the ambulance yet.

"Dad! Can you hear me?" I asked while squeezing his hand. The paramedics were not too happy I was wiggling my way in between, but they didn't look like they were doing anything too important to him right now.

"Yes, Kennedy, I can hear you. Are you OK honey? Are you hurt?" he asked.

"Yeah, Dad, I'm fine, it's you I'm worried about. I heard them say it was your shoulder, are you OK?" I asked him back.

"Yes, yes, I'll be fine, but I wouldn't be if you hadn't rescued me, and your brother. I feel weird saying that again- your brother," his voice faded.

"We have to put him in the ambulance and go now," one paramedic said.

"OK, one second. Dad, did you see we found Natalie? Should I come with you, or follow you in the car?" I asked.

He looked totally confused by my comment of finding Natalie, and just said, "Follow in the car; let these guys do their job. I'll see you at the hospital honey, and thank you. I love you."

"Love you too, Dad."

## CHAPTER 16: WHOLE AGAIN

    The ambulances pulled away, and only a few cop cars were left. Two of the most important people to me were being taken away in ambulances, and it looked like they were going to be fine, but I couldn't get a grasp on the enormity of it all. I also couldn't find Reagan. After all that, and I still couldn't find him!
    I walked up to the nearest cop and asked where he was. He said that he was inside the house with a few other policemen. I didn't really want to go back inside after everything that had just happened. I felt out of place in that house, like a spy. I knew the ins and outs of the house through my visions, and the only time I had been inside was when my brother shot and killed the man he had previously thought was his father. I couldn't imagine what Reagan was probably feeling right now. The only family he had ever known turned out to be a criminal, who shot his biological father, and almost his biological sister, and he was forced to become a murderer, even if it was in self-defense.

I could feel the warm tears start to trickle down my face. I got to the front door, but couldn't force myself to walk in. I waited for ten minutes. Reagan walked out next to a policeman, with only a backpack in hand.

"Reagan?" I said.

"Hey," he responded. This was so awkward, but it wasn't. I had seen this boy grow up- well kind of- never knowing he was my brother. Then, all of a sudden, he rescues both me and my father- *our* father. I felt such gratitude toward him. I was so proud of him for so many things, but we were still strangers. He stopped to look at me, and the cop kept walking toward the cars that were left.

"Are you OK?" I asked him. He still looked tired.

"Yeah, I'm fine, just tired, ya know?" he said quietly.

"Are you going to the hospital?" I asked him.

"Um, I guess. Are you?" he responded. I felt like we were playing twenty questions. My turn.

"Yeah. Dad and Natalie are there, they're going to be okay, but I have to go now."

"Yeah," was all he said. We just stood there awkwardly for a moment. I wasn't sure if I was supposed to offer him a ride or not. Would he even want to go with me? He doesn't know me. What was the proper procedure with all of this? Does the kidnapped boy just go with his real family now? I was so lost.

"You want a ride?" I asked. He started to smile a bit.

"Yes, please." We walked toward my dad's SUV. The police stopped us again and tried to get us both to go to the police station until they could call the Pittsburgh and Philadelphia police to verify this story, and be 100 percent sure about Reagan's identity. The police were not taking no for an answer. I was talking for the both of us, as older sisters do, I imagine, but we were getting nowhere. Reagan stepped up. "Listen, please let us go see our dad and my sister's friend. I am so sure this is my sister, and that was my father. Can't you just figure this out while we are at the hospital? You can have someone come with us," he suggested.

"I guess we could have an officer go with you, but how are you so sure? Apparently, you were only a year old when you were kidnapped, you couldn't possibly remember your family," the officer said back to us. I just looked at Reagan. The officer had made a good point. The only reason I knew this was my brother was because of my dreams. I know parents say they would know their child anywhere, but how hard would it be to not see your child from when he was one until he was fifteen? How could you possibly recognize him from the kid next door?

"Officer, I'm sure," was all Reagan said.

"Yes, but how?" the officer demanded.

"I've dreamt about my sister since I can remember. This is my sister, I would know that face anywhere," he said. I was shocked. He dreamt about me just like I dreamt about him. I wondered if he had dreams about other things as well, like I had with Natalie, or had flashes, or did we just have some weird sibling connection? I had so much to ask him once we were alone.

With Reagan's statement, the officer let us get in our dad's SUV and go to the hospital. We had a police escort that got us there quickly, but also ensured we weren't pulling any funny business. The car ride was pretty quiet, both of us taking everything in, but I did call my mom as soon as we got in the car. I told her about Dad and Natalie, and that Reagan was in the car with me now. She, of course, wanted to speak to him, and he obliged. Their conversation was relatively quick, and most of it was our mom crying and saying she loved him, and him just giving some sort of affirmative response. I hoped that it wouldn't hurt her feelings that he didn't reciprocate "I love you," but he didn't really know us. Once they hung up, I called the Hall's. The police had already gotten in touch with them and they were already on their way to D.C. to meet Natalie at the hospital. It was about 10:30 at night, so they wouldn't be hitting any traffic, but it would still be a few hours until they arrived. They thanked me numerous times for finding Natalie. Mrs. Hall sounded frantic, and I didn't want to keep her on the phone, I just wanted to make sure she had heard the news.

Luckily the hospital wasn't very far away, and just as I was getting off the phone with Mrs. Hall, we were pulling up to the parking lot. The cops escorted us inside and directly to where Natalie was. A nurse came over to us to tell us that our dad was in surgery. He needed to get the bullet removed and have the wound cleaned, but after that, he just needed to relax and recover. They told us they would let us know when he was out of surgery and into a room. I was so thankful that he was going to be OK, and I could see the relief on Reagan's face as well.

"I'm sorry," Reagan said, starting to tear up a little.

"What are you sorry for?" I asked him, kind of sharply actually, wondering where this was coming from.

"Because my dad- I mean- Carl, shot your- I mean our dad." There was a lot of confusion in his voice.

"Reagan, it's not your fault. Come here, sit down," I told him. "None of this is your fault, and Dad's going to be OK, you heard the nurse. He will be fine. And you saved us, remember that part?"

"No, I killed him. I killed the man I thought was my dad. I killed him," he said. He was crying and shaking at this point. I felt so bad for him. This kid was going through so much.

"No, Reagan. You saved our dad, and me. I am so grateful that you came when you did. Carl was going to kill me and Dad. He was. I know that's hard for you, because he was a good dad to you all these years," I told him. He looked up and wiped his tears, his eyes were bright.

"How did you know?" he asked, "because he really was. He loved me, and I loved him. He was a great dad until three days ago."

"I know. I could tell how much he loved you and cared for you. He had something wrong with him, and he had some really bad things happen to him to make him like that. I'll tell you later when this all settles down. But I knew he loved you, because remember how you told the cop back at your house how you always dreamt of me growing up? Well, I have always dreamt of you," I finished.

"You have?" he asked.

"Yes. But to be fair, I didn't know who you were, but I always felt that you were happy, and safe, and loved, and even when I dreamt of you recently, when I saw Carl's face, I could tell he loved you and treated you well."

"He did. He really did. I feel so bad," he told me, being so truthful.

"I know, and I'm sorry you were put in that situation, but you saved us," I told him. I knew this wasn't a good enough response, or one that he deserved, but that was all I could muster at this time. I really did feel bad for him though.

"You saved me, Kennedy. I love you," he said coming out of nowhere. He looked up and leaned in for a hug. It felt weird hugging a stranger, but as soon as I wrapped my arms around my little brother this amazing feeling flooded through me. It wasn't like the jolt I sometimes get with flashes and visions, but it was an immeasurable calmness and lightness. My mind seemed to clear, my heart calmed to a normal beat, and happiness spread through my veins. It was like someone turning on the sunlight while you're lying on the beach and getting a massage. The most relaxing, amazing, indescribably brilliant feeling I have ever felt, and I highly doubt I will ever feel again. Reagan felt it too, and we lingered on our hug.

"I love you too, Reagan," I said back, truly meaning it. I told him I was going to check on Natalie, and he was going to wait there for me.

I walked into Natalie's room and she seemed comfortable enough. She already had the TV on, and she and Nate were gabbing away. If that girl had a little bit of makeup on, and washed her hair, it would be like nothing had ever happened. She still had an IV in her arm giving her fluids, but she looked great. She was antsy because she wanted some real food, she kept saying, and she kept sending Nate to go ask the nurses when she'd get some. Nate would just shake his head and oblige. I held Natalie's hand while she thanked me a million times. I really was sick of hearing the words, but I was thankful too. I was thankful that I had my best friend back, and she was out of harm's way. I was thankful that I had my brother back, even though until recently I didn't even know that I had a brother. I was also so very thankful that my father would be coming out of surgery and would fully recover after all he had been through. So, I let people tell me "thank you" all the while I was thinking how thankful I was indeed.

Nate had told Natalie the whole story from the start, to when we found her, mostly all of my dreams and visions and flashes, and everything else you can think of, so she was excited to recount those events with me. She couldn't believe that I had had those vivid of dreams and flashes. Then I realized I hadn't asked her what had happened that night when Carl took her. I was dying to know, but I didn't want to upset her, so I slowly broached the subject. She seemed receptive and started to chatter away.

"So that night, Kyle and I had just had a fight, so I stormed outside and was hanging with some of those boys, like Tanner and I can't remember who else, but you know who I'm talking about," she started. "Then this guy, Carl, pulls into the driveway and gets out of the car. And I'm like, 'woah, who is this old guy?' so I walk toward him and ask him who he was. And he won't tell me but he is asking for you, Kennedy. So, I'm like, 'Well who the hell are you, that's my best friend.' And he still won't tell me, but he figured you were there, so he tried to walk past me. So, I was like, I'm not going to let this weirdo go find you, so I get in front of him and I'm like, 'Who are you, ya creep?' and he did not like that. He grabbed me by the wrist and flung me to the side. He told me to mind my own business, and that your parents told him you were here and they told him to come pick you up- some family emergency. And I knew your parents would never do that, so I run up to him again, and grabbed his shoulder, and am like, 'Seriously, get the hell out of here before I call the cops, you perv!' And that's when he hit me. I can't believe those drunk guys didn't see what was going on! They are totally worthless. Carl slapped me, and I was shocked. So, I tried to run and he flung me into the side of the hill, in the woods, ya know? That's where you must have found my bracelet, because when I fell, I hit my hand pretty hard on a rock or something. I tried to get up and yell and run away, but he hit me in the head with a beer bottle, I think- something hard- and I got knocked out, because the next thing I remember I was in the back of his car. My mouth was duct taped, my arms were duct taped behind my back, and my feet were too. Then he put me in the shed, and you know the rest pretty much. I was really giving up hope though, Kennedy. It was so weird, because besides the fact that he knocked me out, tied me up, and kidnapped me, Carl seemed like a decent guy. That is totally mental for me to say, I realize, but really, I felt bad for him. He seemed like he had something wrong with him. Did he? Do you know anything about him? I can't believe he had your brother too? What are the freaking odds?" Natalie paused for a second, and I don't think she realized how it all connected because she was exhausted and dehydrated, and had been through a lot, so I let her take a breath and take it all in.

"Actually, I think he was trying to find me that night because he thought Reagan had contacted me. Reagan is so smart, he figured all of it out- that Carl wasn't his real father- and he found an article talking about my family, and he wrote my name down. So, I think Carl was after me to see if Reagan had contacted me, I'm not sure. But you got in his way, and that's why he did that. I'm so sorry, Natalie, he was after me, and you got into this whole mess. I'm so sorry," I told her.

"Kennedy! Shut up! So not your fault, and you saved my ass, girl! Honestly, you are like my super hero best friend, it's awesome!" Natalie said in her usual fantasy world voice. It's so funny that she still seemed so energetic and upbeat after everything she had gone through.

Nate was back, and I wanted to go check on my dad's progress, so I left the room. I tried to tell Nate to tell her to get some sleep, and he just nodded and turned back all his focus on Natalie. A few minutes later, I walked by the room and saw them holding hands and Natalie drifted off to sleep. I always knew they would make a good couple if Natalie just opened up her eyes, and it seemed like she finally was.

Reagan and I waited anxiously for any update on our dad, and the doctor came out after surgery giving us the good news. He told us that our dad had gotten through the surgery very well, the bullet was out and hit no major arteries, and he'd recover very quickly, but was resting now. We were both so relieved. My mom called again and told me she was just a few minutes away, and that she was with Nate's mom, and the Hall's were in front of them. They had all caravanned down. That sounds weird since caravanning is usually reserved for soccer trips and vacations, but they were all coming to the same place to retrieve their respective families, and I was so happy. Reagan and I knew we only had a few more minutes alone before the families arrived.

We sat in silence for a long time, then he looked at me and began to talk. "Remember how you told me you'd explain about Carl? Well, I already know. I saw it on the computer, I saw the article." I had almost forgot. I only knew about the article, because I saw Reagan looking at it. I still wasn't used to everything that I- or we- were capable of doing.

"Oh, yeah, sorry, I forgot, that's how I knew too. I saw you reading on the computer," I told him.

"So, wait, what all did you see me doing?" he asked. I tried to quickly recount everything, all the signs, and dreams, and flashes that I'd had of him and Natalie. He seemed really excited about it all. "So, do you think I can do that stuff too? Like dream about other stuff, or get these flash things?" he asked.

"I guess. You had dreams about me, and that's how mine started," I told him.

"Can you teach me?" he smiled.

"Of course, little bro," I smiled back.

# AFTERWORD

    A lot happened in those action-packed 72 hours. My best friend was kidnapped, then found, thankfully, relatively unscathed. My father was shot in the shoulder, but recovered nicely after surgery. My brother, who was kidnapped fourteen years earlier, had been found at the same place that my best friend was found, and seamlessly integrated into the family he was born into. Those were the main events, but so much else changed too.

    My dad stayed in D.C. for a week to recover from his surgery, and then drove up to Pittsburgh with his wife, and they bought a house one street over. My dad had lost so much time with Reagan that he couldn't bare the thought of being four hours away from his son after all this time. My mother and father's relationship had never been better. I was under no illusion that my father was going to leave Janet, plus I really did like her, but it was nice to have a mom and dad that really got along so we could all be one big family.

Nate and Natalie continued their shocking hospital romance long after that first night that they held hands. Natalie is at Penn State, as planned, and Nate still went to UPenn. They were only about three and a half hours away, and of course they both had cars, so they made sure to visit each other as much as possible. It has been kind of weird that my two best friends are dating, and I often feel like the third wheel whenever they are home and we are all together, and even on our phone conversations, because Natalie is always talking about Nate, and vice versa. I am happy for them though. Kyle got ditched, obviously, but he didn't care much. He moved on quickly to every girl that was still impressed by his captain status on the lacrosse team. Natalie told me she has seen him a few times up at Penn State, but he ignores her, and she is happy to reciprocate that notion. She even told me that she heard he rushed a fraternity up at Penn State and got rejected. Karma.

My mother has continued her friendship with Nate's mom, and they really enjoy themselves. They meet for lunch, and Nate's mom has even invited mine to the country club. My mom feels out of place, or so she says, but she enjoys going. Natalie's parents have even been friendlier with my family, which is nice, and long overdue.

I realized shortly after returning to Pittsburgh that June day, after my world had completely fallen apart, that I couldn't imagine going across the country, far away from my family, just as it was finally being put back together again. I deferred my admission to Colorado, and really just planned on taking a year off, working, and getting to know my little brother. But as chance would have it, the media got their greedy little fingers all over the story of what transpired from prom night, until finding my long lost brother. They, of course, sensationalized it all, made me look like a nut job, and then a heroine, and soon enough, I was getting calls from the University of Pittsburgh. Someone from admissions had heard the story- it was all over the news and in the newspapers- and wanted to offer me admission to the university. Of course I had the grades to get in, but either way, they were more than happy to have such a high profile freshman entering the school. They offered me special housing, where the athletes typically live, but I declined. I had a large, comfy room in the house that I have always considered my home and I was fine with commuting. This way, I was still able to move on with my life and go to college, but I got to be at home with my family- my whole family.

Sometimes I still pinch myself when I get home from class and I hear my mom scurrying in the kitchen, and she tells me that we have to hurry to make it to Reagan's baseball game. It's like all this has been a dream. And my brother is quite the baseball stud, if I do say so myself. He's only a junior, but he's already received mail from some big baseball colleges. Every time I open the mailbox and see a letter from a college addressed to my brother, I can't help but be proud. Reagan was a little reserved with our family at first, but really, considering his whole world had been turned upside down, he did surprisingly well integrating into the life he should have had from the beginning.

The time I knew we really were a family, was when we had our first family fight. It was Christmas, and Reagan, being a typical teenage boy, wanted to ditch out early on Christmas Eve family festivities to go to one of his friend's houses. The entire extended family was over, including my dad and Janet, and her two kids. Their significant others were with them, and even Natalie's and Nate's parents were there. Reagan didn't think it was fair that my two best friends were over, and he had to spend the night without any of his. Mom handled it well, telling him he could invite a friend over, but he pouted and went to his room. We all heard the door slam. My mom looked stunned, and my dad looked a bit mad, but I just smiled. This was exactly how a 16-year-old high school boy was going to act with his family, and it didn't mean we loved him any less, or he us. A few minutes later, Reagan slouched downstairs and apologized to my mom by giving her a hug. I heard him say softly that he had called his buddy, Ryan, but Ryan's mom wouldn't let him leave because it was "family time." Reagan smiled and rejoined our family party.

And lastly, as far as Reagan's and my psychic abilities are concerned, we definitely both have something going on. I still have dreams, although they are few and far between, about something that happens shortly thereafter. I saw that I was going to end up going to college at Pitt, and I actually saw where Reagan is going to pick to go to college. I haven't told him yet, but I wrote it down, so I can prove to him that I knew before he did! Reagan has dreams too, but he's still trying to filter out what dreams are memories, and what might happen in the future.

I tried to teach him how to tap into having flashes, but he hasn't gotten it yet. To be honest, I haven't been able to do many since those crazy three days either. I think that's because my sensitivities and intuition were extremely heightened during that time, because of the direness of the situation. I'm not trying to become a psychic who will read people's futures, or predict the winning lottery number, not at all, but I think it's an interesting quality that I am definitely still looking into, if you know what I mean.

By the way, Reagan is going to choose the University of South Carolina. I've heard they are the defending national champions, or something sporty like that, but don't tell him I knew first!

# About the Author

L.A. Lyons was born and raised in Pittsburgh, Pennsylvania. After graduating from Virginia Tech with a degree in English, she returned to her hometown to obtain her law degree from Duquesne University. Although she loves the law, she has always found her way back to writing. She currently lives in Pittsburgh. This is her first novel.

# Available Titles from Charles Towne Publishing

➢ **Crooked River** by MP Murphy

*With a killer on the loose, bodies disappearing, and time running out, what former FBI agent Jack Francis took as a simple blackmail case soon begins to unravel into a web of deception and greed, as he attempts to retrieve the evidence and protect those close to him from becoming the next victim.*

➢ **The History of Walt Disney Animation**

*An in depth look into the life of Walt Disney and the animation studio he created. Detailed accounts of Disney's animated features are included.* **Edited** *by S.B. Jeffery*

# Coming Soon...

## *Lily in Bloom* by Tammy Andresen

All Charles Towne Publishing books are available at:

Amazon.com

The Kindle Library

And at
www.charlestownepublish.com

Made in the USA
Lexington, KY
10 April 2012